# ABOUT THE AUTHOR

Writer and film-maker Bruno Portier spent twelve years working in Asia making documentaries before returning to France to study for a doctorate in Social Anthropology. He now combines directing documentary films with writing feature film scripts and ethnological articles. He is working on his next novel, a sequel to *This Flawless Place Between*.

*This*

# FLAWLESS

*Place*

# BETWEEN

# BRUNO PORTIER

ONEWORLD

A Oneworld Book

First published in English by Oneworld Publications 2012
First published as *Bardo, Le Passage* by
Éditions Florent Massot, in 2009

Hardback Edition ISBN 978-1-85168-850-0
Travel Edition ISBN 978-1-85168-926-2
Ebook ISBN 978-1-85168-851-7

Front cover design credit © Leo Nickolls
Typeset in Jayvee, Trivandrum, India
Printed in Great Britain by TJ International

Oneworld Publications
185 Banbury Road
Oxford OX2 7AR
England

Learn more about Oneworld. Join our mailing list to
find out about our latest titles and special offers at:
www.oneworld-publications.com

# Acknowledgements

I wish to thank Denis Héroux, Stéphanie Röckmann, François and Anne-Marie Portier, Matthieu Ricard, Karine Frechet, Elsa Vasseur, Zsuzsanna Hadju, Gül Isikveren and Florent Massot for their reading, comments and support during the writing of this book.

Author's Note
on The Tibetan Book of
the Dead

# The Tibetan Book of the Dead

The original title of *The Tibetan Book of the Dead* is *Bardo Thödol Chenmo*, which can be translated as 'liberation through hearing during the *bardo*'. *Bardo* means intermediate state, intermediate world or interval; the *bardos* are periods of crisis and profound doubt that a person undergoes in the course of their existence. These transitory periods offer exceptional opportunities for raised awareness and liberation. According to Tibetan schools of Buddhism, a complete life cycle contains between four and six *bardos*. The first is the *bardo* that continues from the moment of conception to the moment of death. The second, one aspect of this, is the dream state. The third is the *bardo* experienced by those who practise meditation. Death and the days that follow it contain the next three. One occurs during the dying process: the *bardo* of the moment before death. The next is the *bardo* of reality, also called the *dharmata*,[1] which offers a moment of 'flawless'

---

[1] *Dharmata* means essence or intrinsic nature.

ix

luminosity, possible for everyone, but recognised only by some. The last is the *bardo* of rebirth or becoming, which leads to the next rebirth.

*The Tibetan Book of the Dead* describes the experience of the deceased from the moment of death until rebirth. In fact, to quote Sogyal Rinpoche, it is a sort of 'travel guide'. The descriptions contained in the book are astonishingly precise. Unfortunately, for readers uninitiated in Tibetan Buddhism it takes many hours of study to understand it, as the book draws on an enormous wealth of symbolism. It is therefore helpful to read analyses and explanations by other authors[2] to make the best sense of the text.

*This Flawless Place Between* was born of a desire to make *The Tibetan Book of the Dead* accessible to a wider readership, and, to inspire readers to turn to translations and studies of the original text. The novel follows, as scrupulously as possible, the different stages of the book and transcribes the key moments into a narrative rooted in a world more familiar to Western readers. Particular care has been taken to respect the meaning and primary purpose of the book: offering guidance to the dying, helping them to attain enlightenment by liberating themselves from *samsara* – the cycle of existence –

---

[2] For those wanting to read further, a bibliography can be found at the end of this book.

or, failing this, to orientate themselves towards the best new life possible.

*The Tibetan Book of the Dead* emphasises the weight of our actions in this life and the effects they can have on our future states. However, beyond the positive or negative influence of our *karma*[3] on our lives and deaths, there are other opportunities.[4] The book stresses that every *bardo* offers possibilities for liberation. Even if one does not attain enlightenment, it is still possible to direct our rebirths towards the most favourable outcome.

Ideally, the book should be studied before death; but it is also read to the dying and the dead, who can understand its meaning whatever their culture, language or religion, regardless of whether they speak Tibetan or understand Buddhist symbolism. The dead and the dying are gifted with exceptional perception during the days that immediately follow their deaths.

---

[3] The term *karma* signifies action and denotes the totality of a being's acts past, present and future. *Karma* has a dominant impact in terms of cause or consequence on our cycles of being, our lives and deaths included.

[4] In the course of his youth, Milarepa, one of Tibet's most important religious leaders, caused the deaths of dozens of people. This did not prevent him from achieving enlightenment and becoming a great spiritual master.

*The Tibetan Book of the Dead* is universal. It is an intrinsically hopeful work that seeks to improve the condition of all beings, life after life, regardless of their belief systems or the actions they have committed.

This Flawless Place Between

A wild rabbit sits in yellowing grass, surrounded by tufts of dandelion. Ears straining towards the sky, it turns its head and glances first left, then right. Behind it, a group of youngsters begin to explore. Carefree, oblivious, two of them wander across the white line dividing greenery from asphalt. A rumbling sound catches the attention of the adult; it cocks its head, staring blankly into the distance. It seems as unafraid as the kits at their games. The rumble grows steadily into a low roar and then explodes in a deafening blast. The young rabbits freeze; a powerful gust of wind ruffles their grey fur. A few metres ahead of them, six enormous tyres squeal off the asphalt. Crouched low to the ground, the pair on the runway watch the monster swoop past. As for the others, they have already returned to what they were doing.

\* \* \*

John F. Kennedy Airport, New York, USA. Flights scroll down the overhead board. Announcements crackle from loudspeakers. Baggage carts collide, spilling bags and suitcases. The departures area bustles with people: businessmen, housewives, backpackers, groups of pensioners, restless teen-agers, policemen, air hostesses. Some eat, others drink, others read, make phone calls, chat.

In the midst of the chaos is Anne, a woman in her thirties wearing a leather biker jacket, waiting in the line at check-in counter 49, destination Kolkata. Kneeling on the tiled floor in a gap hemmed in by the legs of other passengers, she rifles through her backpack. On her right cheek is a small beauty spot. Her eyes are chestnut brown, like her hair, which is short and neatly cut.

'Where did I put my damn passport?'

Standing over her is a young man, a few years older. He too is dressed in leather, and has very short brown hair. His name is Evan, Anne's part-ner. He laughs.

'We're off to a good start.'

A couple in their sixties stand to the side. These are Anne's parents, Rose and John.

John holds in his arms an eighteen-month-old girl. She is wearing a bright red cycle helmet with

4

large black holes that look like the spots on a lady-bug. This is Lucy, their granddaughter, Anne's child.

Rose smiles, amused, as she watches Anne going through her backpack.

'Well, Evan, you wanted an adventure. With Anne you won't be disappointed!'

'Thanks for the encouragement!'

At their feet, Anne feverishly pulls various things out of her pack and dumps them on the floor. Amongst them are photographs. In one of them, Anne poses beside an elegant well-dressed man in his fifties, holding a newborn Lucy in his arms.

The passengers ahead of them at the desk collect their boarding passes.

'Thank you.'

The woman responds with an obliging smile. 'You're welcome. Have a nice trip.'

'Ah, found it!'

Still on her knees, Anne proudly flourishes her passport.

'It was in the guidebook.'

'Thank goodness.'

Evan takes the passport, turns and hands it to the check-in assistant.

Rose watches, concerned, as Anne hastily repacks her things.

'Have you remembered the anti-malarial tablets? I don't want you coming back with malaria. And –'

John cuts her off.

'Rose, don't start that again, please. They're grown-ups.'

Anne nods in agreement, fastens her backpack and gets up.

'Mom, Evan's a nurse, remember? And besides, there's no malaria in the Himalayas.'

'Oh, all right! Don't get at me. I worry, that's all. It's normal to worry about your children. You worry too, don't you?'

John intervenes again.

'Rose, I asked you to stop.'

Anne drags her bag to the counter, lifts it and drops it onto the conveyer belt to be weighed. The passengers behind her move up a few steps, treading on the forgotten photograph of the man holding Lucy as a baby.

'Mom, you're right. But I've got good reasons to worry.'

Anne lifts Lucy out of her father's arms and gives her a big kiss on the cheek, holding her close.

'Don't forget to shut the stair gate upstairs and to put her helmet on the moment she gets up, okay?'

John sighs. Rose frowns.

'Anne, you've already told us a thousand times, and what's more –'

She extracts a typewritten sheet of paper from her pocket, playfully brandishing it in front of her daughter's face.

'– you've written it down for us too!'

Anne rocks Lucy in her arms, as if she needed to calm her.

'Like that's going to stop you doing whatever you feel like.'

Turning back from the counter, Evan interrupts them.

'Anne, do you want a window seat?'

'Sure, why not?'

Anne cradles her daughter, who is frowning at the adults' argument.

'Don't be sad, sweetie. It's hard for me too, you know. But I can't take you out there. You're too little . . .'

Pressed to her face, Lucy squints up at her.

'. . . And then we'll be home very soon. Three weeks isn't very long, you know. Grandma and Grandpa will look after you, you'll see. You're going to have a whale of a time . . .'

Anne hugs her daughter, kisses her again and murmurs in her ear, '. . . I'll bring you back a beautiful present.'

The little girl clings to her mother's neck. Rose joins them and affectionately strokes Lucy's back.

'Don't worry, Anne. Everything will be fine.

Anne smiles, looking sad.

'I know. Thanks. I'll call you as soon as we've arrived.'

* * *

Four in the morning. Kolkata airport. A dilapidated red bus trundles down the asphalt, bathed in the dirty yellow glow of the sodium lights. Its windows are open. Inside, the travellers are squashed together like sardines. Shaken and jolted, exhausted by the journey, they are sticky with sweat. It's still pitch black, and already getting muggy.

Anne and Evan are in the back, crushed between an Indian family and a group of retired tourists. They stare out of the side windows, stunned. Anne takes deep breaths. She's trying to keep at bay the rising nausea brought on by the acrid smell seeping from the grey hair pressed in her face.

The bus halts, its doors opening. Free at last, the horde of jostling passengers bursts out and hurries into the starkly lit hall, in pursuit of luggage. Trailing behind, Anne and Evan rejoin the crowd thronging about the empty baggage carousel. Anne takes out her mobile phone and switches it on. The phone bleeps a few times, then turns itself off.

'Shit, my battery's dead. Will you wait for me

here? I have to phone Mom to let her know we've arrived okay.'

'Fine.'

Anne walks off, leaving Evan to wriggle through the tangle of passengers and crippled trolleys.

She comes to a large hall with pale blue walls. The floor is strewn with sleeping people. Faulty wiring makes the fluorescent lights flicker intermittently. The place is silent, save for the occasional snore. Anne, feeling ill at ease, picks her way between the sleepers until she reaches a row of wooden telephone booths along a wall next to the toilets. They're all stripped have except the last, which houses an old rotary dial telephone. Anne steps inside and lifts the handset. There's no tone. She hangs up and looks around. There, a few metres away and scarcely visible, a tiny opening in the wall: a public telephone office. Behind the counter, on a bare worktop, a cigarette smoulders in an ashtray, abandoned by a smoker nowhere in sight. Anne turns again and looks around her. Everyone is asleep, wrapped in cloths on the bare floor, wedged between linen sacks, sprawled across plastic chairs. Suddenly, a slammed door echoes through the hall. Anne jumps, startled. A smartly dressed young Indian walks out of the toilets, fastening his flies. Anne rushes over.

'Sir?'

The Indian, embarrassed, hastily tucks his shirt into his trousers and turns to her.

'Yes, madam?'

'Excuse me. I'm looking for whoever's in charge of this telephone office.'

Anne points towards the gap in the wall. The Indian clears his throat.

'That is myself.'

He straightens his tie and returns to his post with a dignified air. Anne follows him. He sits on his chair behind the counter and retrieves his cigarette.

'You are wishing to make a call, isn't it?'

Anne nods, amused.

'Er . . . yes, I do.'

'Is it you are wishing to make an international call, madam?'

'Yes, please.'

'This is the telephone. Please to dial the number.'

He extracts from a drawer an ultra-modern handset and places it on the counter. Anne picks it up, punches the number into the digital keys and waits. The operator stares at her unabashedly. She gives him a little embarrassed smile. The number rings at last. Anne sighs with relief. The operator's stare turns lascivious and Anne sighs again, this time in exasperation. She turns around. The line keeps ringing. Nobody answers. In the hall, the bodies lie unmoving, as though abandoned. Anne cannot help thinking of a morgue. She begins to worry.

* * *

The taxi hoots again and again. Dawn is breaking over the city and flooding the streets with a bluish light. A thin mist rises from the ground, giving the scene an air of unreality. Along the roadside is a succession of shacks made of planks and recycled metal drums. Here and there, brightly coloured saris are drying. Half-dressed women rinse shampoo out of their long, black hair. Cooking pots steam over small wood fires. Children, scarcely awake, wander aimlessly, brushing their teeth with sticks, while the elderly sit and sip their tea, huddled in thick brown blankets. Cars and lorries swerve by, narrowly missing hand-drawn carts, rickshaws, cows, pedestrians.

Anne and Evan are in the taxi, on the back seat. Evan tries to reassure Anne.

'Stop worrying. We'll find a power socket at the rental agency and you'll call her again, okay?'

He pats her thigh affectionately.

'Look out the window. We're in Kolkata. Isn't it incredible?'

The driver hoots a warning to a group of

schoolgirls in impeccably ironed uniforms, who run squealing into the gutter.

'To think, yesterday we were on the other side of the world, eating shepherd's pie in the hospital cafeteria.'

Anne looks pensively out of the window.

\* \* \*

Inside the small, poorly lit rental agency, Anne shows her phone and charger to the fat, dark-skinned proprietor comfortably ensconced deep in a seventies' office chair. The deafening noise of the street and of the fan above their heads forces them to speak loudly.

'My phone battery, could I charge it? I need to make an urgent call.'

The proprietor looks at her with a grimace.

'I am very sorry, madam. That is not the plug we are using. It is another plug you will be needing.'

'Then could I use your phone?'

The Indian winces again. 'You are wishing to make a local call, is it?'

'No, I need to call my mother in the States.'

'Ah. Most regrettable. The international line, it is not working. Impossible.'

Anne loses her temper. 'For God's sake!'

'Anne, calm down!' Beside her, Evan is poring

over a map of north-east India. 'We'll buy an adaptor on our way out and you can make your call then.'

Anne gets up, takes a few steps and collapses onto a black imitation leather couch at the back of the office.

Evan returns to what he had been saying, 'How many days does it take to get to Gangtok?'

'It is very difficult to know this. It is depending on the road. We are having very heavy monsoon last year. Perhaps the road it has not been repaired.'

He pretends to think, takes a handkerchief from his trouser back pocket and pats his sweat-sheened brow.

'Mmm. Three, four days, it is possible.'

'Okay. Are there gas stations all along the route?'

'Oh no. As far as Siliguri there are many, many stations. The road it is very busy. But after Siliguri, it is necessary you must carry a petrol can.'

Evan sits up in his chair and stretches, his arms in the air.

'Right. Can you think of anything else, Anne?'

Sitting motionless on the couch beneath a faded Bengali tourism poster, Anne stares straight ahead and shakes her head. Outside in the street, behind the tinted plastic coating peeling off the window, a little girl of about ten carries an emaciated baby on her hip. She taps relentlessly on the glass with her free hand, then lifts it to her mouth to indicate hunger. Anne cannot look away. The owner notices. Rising, he pushes open the door and waves the girl away, yelling a few words in Hindi followed by a 'Shhhttt' better suited to chasing off a dog than a human being. Anne gets up, walks past him and leaves without saying a word.

'Madam, madam, please, do not give her anything.'

Anne dashes across the busy road, followed by the little girl. Car horns blare. Anne pays them no attention. She jumps onto the opposite pavement and strides into a shack serving as a public telephone kiosk.

'Please, can I make a call here?'

Startled by the interruption, the operator hurries to turn on the light and the ceiling fan before starting the timer and handing the telephone to Anne.

'Please.'

Anne dials the number. The phone rings once, twice, three times.

'Hello?'

Anne recognises her mother's voice instantly.

'Mom! Where on earth were you?'

'Where was I? What do you mean?'

'I tried to call you from the airport when we landed but no one answered. I've been sick with worry.'

There is a short, careful silence on the other end of the line.

'Listen, Anne. I'm sorry. We must have been outside the garden. You simply have to start trusting people again. You can't live with this sort of stress.'

Anne lets out a sigh.

'I know, I know. I'm sorry.'

'You don't have to apologise. Just use your trip to try to relax, all right?'

Anne smiles.

'All right. How's Lucy?'

Rose's tone brightens.

'She's doing great. She's in bed. She's so funny. I must tell you what happened this afternoon in the park . . .'

\* \* \*

The room is dark; there is a single window with a blind. The paint on the walls is greenish and faded. A clapped-out air conditioner bulges from the wall. Its blades, whirring at full speed, smack against the rusty protective grille, making a regular clicking sound that blends with the religious chanting from a distant radio. From another room, Anne calls out to Evan cheerfully, 'Listen, I think I'm going to give up on the leather. It's much too hot.'

Water drips steadily from the air conditioner's

15

metal casing, following a chalky yellow line down the wall. The thin trickle passes within a few centimetres of an electric socket and lands on a greying pillowcase, forming a steadily expanding damp spot.

'Evan, can you hear me?'

Evan's head is on the pillow. He is asleep, his hair wet and perspiration trickling from his temples. A door opens suddenly at the other end of the room. Anne steps naked from the bathroom, rubbing her hair with a towel.

'Evan, get up! It's late.'

Evan groans and turns over in bed. Anne inspects her body in the dresser mirror and sees, reflected, Evan unmoving on the sheet.

'Evan. Look at me!'

She throws her towel in the air, spreads her arms majestically and offers her body to his gaze. He doesn't budge. Anne turns on him roughly.

'Hey! Come on! Wake up! You've been nagging me for months to go on holiday, just the two of us, and now you're sleeping it away! Is this the grand adventure you promised me?'

Evan gingerly opens one eye. Anne pirouettes, flaunting herself at him. Evan gives a hint of a smile.

'But I'll wake you up, you'll see!'

She leaps on him with a yelp.

* * *

16

A violent kick strikes the bony flanks of a stray dog, sending the animal off yapping in pain. A tea towel over his shoulder, the twelve-year-old waiter bounds up the steps that separate the teashop from the side street. Anne and Evan are seated at the entrance, watching the dog hobbles off into the crowd. With a backpack strapped to it, their motorbike, a gleaming Enfield Bullet 500, is parked just below them.

An outstretched arm sets a tray on the table. The young waiter is joyful, his accent heavy.

'A very good day to you! Have a good breakfast!'

On the tray there are two chipped cups filled with a light brown liquid, a saucer with a tablespoon's worth of blood-red purée, a pot of greyish sugar and two oily plates on which float a couple of fried eggs and a slice of burnt, grease-soaked toast. Anne looks at the tray, nauseated. Evan bursts out laughing at the expression on her face.

'Mmm, this looks delicious!'

Anne lifts her head.

'Just what I was about to say.'

Evan continues to smile at her. 'Woo-hoo! We're in India, remember. Look around you.'

'It's not a reason to get ill.' Anne lifts the saucer and sniffs the contents. 'I think it might be ketchup.'

Evan grabs a plate, lifts it like a holy relic and devoutly places it on the table in front of him.

He takes a soggy piece of toast and slowly dips it into the egg yolk, which bursts, oozes and blends with the oil. Stirring the mess with relish, he lifts the dripping toast to his mouth, moaning with pleasure.

'Mmm-mm, it's good! You should try it.'

Anne makes a face. Evan laughs and spits a formless mass into his plate.

'Oh, you're disgusting!'

Evan coughs, chuckling.

'Sorry.'

He takes another bite of his toast. Mouth full, he says, 'Come on, eat. It's deliciously local.'

Anne shakes her head despairingly.

'I'm sure it's practically caviar compared to some of the things you've eaten, but I just don't have your experience. Or stomach.'

She lifts a teacup and sips warily. She gags instantly and Evan again erupts with laughter.

\* \* \*

The leaves of the trees filter a myriad dazzling lights. In the shadow of a row of eucalyptus, a group of naked Jain monks slowly advance, carefully sweeping the road before their feet. An Enfield Bullet roars past them, raising a cloud of dust. On the motorbike, Anne and Evan are wearing headphones in place of helmets. Their leather jackets are wide open. Tilting back her head, Anne stretches out her arms and flaps them like a bird, while in front of her Evan nods his head to the music as he drives. Sheaves of wheat are spread along the roadside, past which nonchalant youths stroll hand in hand, and a peasant pedals a bicycle piled high with poultry-filled cages. Evan honks his horn before overtaking him. Very close by, a second horn sounds, startling Anne, who instantly lowers her arms to grip Evan about the waist. A truck overflowing with hay overtakes and pulls in abruptly in front of them, narrowly avoiding a bus coming the other way. The truck hurtles on at full speed, skimming past a group of elderly women resting by the side of the road. A little further on, men are piling up the load of an overturned pickup truck onto a cart. Anne turns as they pass the scene. Near the wreck, in the ditch, a body lies beneath a bloodstained sheet. A few crows hop around the corpse. Nobody seems to be paying it any attention. Anne cannot bring herself to look away. As the motorbike speeds on, the crashed truck rapidly fades from view.

* * *

Her eyeballs move under closed lids, fleetingly swelling the thin membrane of skin. Bare feet are sliding roughly along a tightrope. Eyes shut, Anne moves unsteadily forward, balanced on a cord wound tightly between two enormous trees that straddle a road. Above her, Lucy is smiling. She floats in the air like a helium balloon. Anne grips her by the heel to keep her balance. Distant voices call to her.

'Anne! Anne!'

Far, far below, her parents, tiny and barely visible, with Evan and Henry, the man from the photograph, are waving frantically to warn her of some danger. Anne opens her eyes, the distance looming below her, and she begins to wobble. She loosens her hold on Lucy's foot and the girl floats away. Anne tips and falls, screaming, at first plummeting like a stone, then turning and floating softly like a leaf. She lands gently on a bloodstained sheet held out by the group below and suddenly rebounds into the air at lightning speed. In an instant she is level with her daughter floating upwards. She fastens her arms round her, refusing to let her escape. A threatening roar surges up around them.

Anne wakes with a start on a rope bed. Close by a truck engine revs up in the darkness. Two large, menacing eyes are painted on the bumper at the back; below them dangle a lemon and a baby's shoe. Anne is by the side of the road in the truckers' lay-by, under a corrugated-iron awning lit murkily by neon strips suspended on string. Besides Evan fast asleep next to her, there is no one to be seen; the place seems deserted. Reeling from her nightmare, Anne yanks her backpack from under the bed and opens a side pocket. She digs out her telephone and dials. The signal is good. She waits, anxiously. Rose picks up. Before she can utter a word, Anne says, 'Mom?'

'Anne?'

'Yes, it's me. Is Lucy all right? I've just had a horrible dream. She was floating up into the sky away from me and I was clinging on to her to try and keep her back. Has anything happened?'

There's an awkward pause. 'Lucy's fine. Don't worry. But it's odd you dreamt that. We had a little accident earlier today. She banged her head against a radiator; we're just back from the hospital and she's got two tiny little stitches. But it's nothing, there's nothing to worry about.'

Anne begins to scream. 'I knew it! I knew it!'

Evan awakes with a jolt.

'You hadn't put her helmet on, had you?'

'Well, yes, but no. She was just getting out of the bath. She was practising walking, holding onto the rim of the bathtub, when she slipped on the tiles. But like I say –'

Anne cuts her mother off. 'Did the doctor do an MRI?'

21

'No, it was nothing. They said it wasn't worth –'

Anne, hysterical, interrupts again. 'It *is* worth it! You know her history! You ask him for an MRI immediately or I'll come straight back and do it myself!'

Anne bursts into tears.

'Ask for an MRI right away, please, I'm begging you. She's in danger. I saw it in my dream.'

Evan sits up.

'Anne, take it easy. What's going on?'

Anne is sobbing so much she can barely speak. 'It's Lucy . . . She's had an accident.'

'Pass me the phone. Hi, Rose, it's Evan. What's going on?'

At the other end of the line, Rose is beginning to cry. 'It's Lucy. She fell and knocked her head in the bathroom . . .' She sniffs. 'It's nothing serious but, you know . . . Anne is so anxious since the accident. And for John and me . . . she just expects too much.'

'Have you taken her to see the neurologist?'

'Of course we did. We've just come back from there. He says it's nothing, but Anne's insisting we get an MRI!'

'Then do it. It won't do any harm, and it will make everybody feel better.'

There's a pause. Rose swallows. 'All right. You're right. Tell Anne we're going right away. We'll call you afterwards.'

'Thank you.' Evan hangs up. 'They're going back to the hospital for an MRI.'

Anne is crying, curled up miserably on her bed. Evan takes her into his arms and rocks her.

'She'll call us as soon as they've got the results.' He kisses her neck tenderly. 'Is that better? What was your dream?'

\* \* \*

Early in the morning, the sky is a limpid blue, flawless and cold. Anne and Evan are on their motorbike, wearing helmets. With her shirt flapping in the breeze, Anne looks over the bewitching countryside without seeing it. Fields blanketed in flowers vie with verdant rice paddies. A few women clothed in brightly coloured saris cross the paddies carrying pitchers and basins on their heads, nonchalantly swaying their hips. Further down in the valley, prayer flags are strung between pine trees. Evan nudges Anne's thigh, pointing them out. The motorbike disappears around a curve.

\* \* \*

The sound of the bike engine melds with the shouts of children. Anne and Evan slowly advance through the main street of the village. Despite the dozen or so Indian and Tibetan children running and shrieking behind them, the atmosphere is thick, heavy, almost tangible. In front of a row of concrete shops overflowing with produce, customers and shopkeepers alike have stopped in their tracks, their heads turning silently, synchronised, to watch the foreigners pass.

\* \* \*

Evan is sitting on an upturned crate, surrounded by a flock of laughing children. He is eating a large and very ripe mango. Thick, orange juice drips along his forearm; Evan slurps it, fluttering his eyelids in exaggerated bliss. The children laugh wildly. In front of Evan is a carrom board; on the other side sits his opponent, a ten-year-old Tibetan boy. Peacock-proud, the boy haughtily sizes Evan up before striking the red puck. It hits the wooden edge, ricochets and knocks a white puck, which slides neatly into a little cloth pouch in a corner of the board. The children leap into the air, screaming their champion on. Amid the shouts a telephone sounds in the distance. Evan raises his eyes.

Sitting apart in the full sun falling on the steps of a shop, Anne hurriedly puts down the bottle of local cola she was drinking and grabs at the mobile phone on her knee.

'Hello?'

Evan watches her out of the corner of his eye.

'What's that? I can't hear you very well.'

Anne claps her left hand over her free ear and raises her voice.

'Nothing . . . Are you sure? You're not just saying that?'

Focused on Anne, Evan strikes the red puck carelessly. The violent flick he gives with his finger causes him to yelp in pain and shake his hand, as the children around him respond with more delighted howls of laughter. Automatically Anne gets up and turns her back to shield herself from the noise. She is now flanked by strings of dusty sachets hanging from the front of the shop: crisps, sweets, betel spices, shampoo, detergent, aspirin, condoms.

She shouts, 'Great. Can you put her on a minute?'

Anne turns around again, relieved. Rooted in front of the store, a little Tibetan girl watches her closely.

'Hello, my darling! Can you hear me?' Anne listens to the babbling of her daughter. 'I love you. Can you hear me? I love you.'

The Tibetan girl draws slowly towards her. Anne gives her a complicit wink.

'Yes, I heard her. Thanks so much.'

The little girl has stopped in front of Anne. She

puts out her hand and carefully caresses the hairs on Anne's forearm. Anne smiles at her.

'All right. I'll call you back in two days. Yes, same time as today. Love you.'

The red puck strikes two sides of the carrom board before hitting the last white disc, which flies out into the net. The king of carrom throws his slender arms up in victory. Evan takes a sweet out of his pocket and hands it over with a vanquished look. The other kids swarm over him as Evan stands up chuckling, passing round handfuls of sweets. Anne goes up to him, a broad smile on her face.

'She's doing fine.'

'You see, I told you! That's wonderful news. So can we get on with our journey now?'

* * *

The sun is high. The motorbike zooms by, sinking into the heat haze that shimmers above the asphalt. It slows suddenly, stopping. Evan puts a foot down and cuts the engine. Anne cranes her head round his shoulder.

'What's the matter?'

'I think I must've eaten something that disagreed with me. Hang on a sec.'

Taking off his helmet, he gets off the bike, grabs a roll of toilet paper from the backpack and hurries into the bushes.

Anne studies their surroundings. The landscape all around them is arid and unwelcoming: yellow earth, brown thorny scrub, littered with grey stones. A few dozen metres ahead, the road divides, forking in two. There are no road signs. Anne frowns.

'Evan? Is Rabang to the left or the right?'

Evan groans from behind his bush. 'I don't know, do I? Take a look at the map.'

Anne gazes at the junction. A young woman in a bright red sari with a bundle of firewood on her head crosses the road and sets off down a dirt track.

'Excuse me!'

The young woman turns gracefully. The vermilion dot between her dark eyebrows sets off her brown eyes, the amber lustre of her skin and the dazzling white of her teeth. Anne hurriedly gets off the bike, removes her helmet and catches up with her.

'Excuse me. Which way is Rabang?'

The young woman doesn't understand. She smiles and nods, waves to Anne and turns away. Anne runs after her and points to the junction.

'Rabang?'

Evan emerges from the bush, buckling his belt, and returns to the bike. The young Indian woman looks briefly at the fork in the road, then turns to Anne.

'Robang?'

Rabang, Robang, Anne isn't sure.

'Er . . . yeah. Robang.'

From a distance, Evan sees the young woman point down the track in the direction she came from, wave to Anne a second time and continue on her way. Anne comes back and casts Evan an inquiring glance. Sitting on the bike some twenty metres away, he responds with a doubtful pout and tenderly massages his belly. Anne signals behind him. An aged Tibetan is sitting at the side of the road beside a chorten[5] of piled stones.

'I'll go and ask him.'

Evan walks around the bike, opens a side pouch, takes out a road map and goes to speak the old man. With a prayer wheel in his hand and his torso slightly bowed, the old man sways, softly murmuring his prayers.

'Excuse me?'

The old man gives a start, lifts his head and smiles at Evan.

'Good afternoon. We're trying to get to Robang.'

Evan shows him the map and points to Rabang. The old man seems not to understand. Evan persists, pronouncing the two syllables of the name.

---

[5] A religious structure commemorating a death or the Buddha.

'Roo bang – do you know it?'

The old man takes the map from Evan's hands and holds it at various angles. Standing by the motorbike, Anne watches worriedly. The old man carefully examines the map upside-down. Suddenly, joyfully, he looks at Evan.

'Rabang?'

'Yes, Rabang, that's right.'

The old man points along the same dirt track the young woman had indicated. Anne turns her head towards the path and shields her eyes. She cannot see the end of it in the low sun's blinding light.

\* \* \*

The motorbike flashes out of the white glare. It climbs a steep, stony path up the flank of a mountain. Shaken by the bumping on the back of the bike, Anne holds tightly onto Evan while looking out over the valley. Down below, broken by a line of cypress trees, are strips of wheat crossing the terraced mountainside, a thousand golden steps catching the light. The bike strains towards the summit. All around them, snow-capped peaks are bathed in the orange rays of the setting sun. Anne taps Evan on the shoulder.

'Stop a minute?'

Evan stops the bike. Anne slumps from the seat, tosses her helmet on a carpet of lichen and improvises a few gymnastic movements to loosen her stiffened legs.

'That's a relief!'

Evan also dismounts and removes his helmet, admiring the view.

'God, it's beautiful.'

Dreamily they sit side by side.

'Why don't we spend the night here?'

Evan turns, incredulous.

'Uh, I think I'd rather sleep in an actual bed, if you don't mind. I've been driving for eight hours, I'm exhausted and I've got a queasy stomach. We can't be very far from Rabang. You remember that lovely little hotel that's in the guidebook?'

A moment passes before Anne shakes her head and turns to him winningly.

'Nobody's expecting us. We've got plenty of anti-diarrhea tablets, a sleeping bag, water, even food. Are you sure you don't want to sleep here with me, cuddled up in our sleeping bag?'

'My darling, I have never been more positive.'

Anne lies on her back, hands under her head.

'Oh well, that's too bad. The sunrise would have been amazing.'

Anne closes her eyes and breathes deeply. Not a sound. All is still. Evan looks at his watch.

'Right, let's get a move on. It'll be dark in two hours.'

Anne ignores him.

'How about a little Bach to wake us up?'

Eyes still closed, Anne sighs, a smile on her lips.

'You and your Bach. I should never have got you to listen to it.'

Evan looks away, tired.

'Fine then. We don't have to if you don't want to.'

Anne opens her eyes and laughs at his weary expression. She catches him by the arm and tips him backwards, climbing on top of him to smother him with little kisses.

'I know . . . we don't . . . have to . . .'

Evan relents for a few moments, before breaking away, briefly hugging her tightly and jumping to his feet.

'Come on, up you get. We can pursue this at the hotel.'

He heads back to the motorbike. Anne remains supine, her eyes taking in the sky: not a cloud in sight. Behind her, the engine starts up. She sighs, rises, picks up her helmet and strides towards the bike shouting, 'Let's go!'

The echo ricochets around the high rocky slopes.

* * *

A great cloud of dust blushes purple in the sunset as the motorbike hurtles along a steep track beside a ravine. Seated at the rear, Anne has both arms wrapped around Evan, her cheek resting on his shoulder, helmet off and headphones on. She is deep in the intoxicating presto of a violin sonata by Johann Sebastian Bach. Her eyes see the landscape transformed by speed, forms and shapes melting into abstract lines, multicoloured and shimmering. Evan is sitting up straight. Hands gripping the handlebars, his feet propped on the footrests, all his attention is on the road in front of him. The Enfield zigzags, nimbly avoiding the loose stones and potholes on the rutted dirt track.

Around the bend a figure steps into the dappled sunlight. Evan swerves sharply. Narrowly skating past the silhouette, the motorbike slips and skids on the loose surface of the mountain road. Evan releases the brake in an attempt to regain control. The motorbike straightens up a little, but too late. The rear wheel is spinning over the chasm, and they hurtle backwards into the precipice.

Anne is thrown off, her headphones torn from her head. Without a cry, her eyes shut, she tumbles, lit by the fire of the setting sun. Her arms, spread wide, embrace the air that swells her white shirt and whistles through her hair. Wheeling and turning, cut loose of her weight, she flies, free, independent, solitary. Her head is empty, void of external images, external sounds. Only her breath, calm and even, cradles her tranquillity.

What if this lasted forever?

But Anne is out of time. Already she is reaching the end of her fall. Her limbs stiffen, anticipating the impact.

. . . It's so good . . .

She breathes in.

. . . Make the most of it . . .

She breathes out.

. . . One moment longer . . .

She breathes in.

. . . Just one mome –

In a fraction of a second, her body crashes, a dislocated mass at the bottom of the ravine. Her skull strikes a rock, bounces loosely, thuds back against the stone and lies still.

# The Bardo of the Moment of Death

Oil drips from the broken crankcase onto the hot cylinder, where it sizzles and burns. The Enfield lies prone beside a skeletal tree. The two safety helmets, intact and still tied to the chrome luggage rack, loll in the dust. Around the wreck lie clothes, a bag of toiletries, camping gear, CDs, the contents of the backpacks spilled and scattered. Evan is lying amid the debris. Stunned, in shock, he shakily lifts his head. They have landed on a rocky outcrop jutting from the sheer precipice, about thirty metres below the road. The ground is grey, rocky, sterile, with a few pines and thorns bushes and not one blade of grass. A blue-jeaned leg is sticking out from behind an acacia tree. It belongs to Anne.

'Anne, are you okay?'

She doesn't answer. Evan calls her again, louder. 'Anne!'

No response. Evan gets up to go to her, but howls with pain as soon as he puts weight on his foot. He falls, screaming, gripping his leg with both hands.

An old Tibetan peasant scurries down the slope, waving his arms.

'Wait!' he shouts in Tibetan. 'Don't move! I'm coming to help you.'

He hurries towards the motionless Anne. Her limbs sprawl across the rock, abandoned in the chaos of the fall. The rips in her shirt expose the rough graze on her right breast. Her bloody cheek rests on the stone. Her half-open eyelids flutter in irregular, mechanical spasms, like a series of Morse code signals. Her expression is frozen, empty and serene. The old Tibetan's face appears above her. His skin is tanned, grooved with deep wrinkles. An antique pair of glasses sits on his flat nose, one of the arms held on by a sticking plaster now black with age. His large eyes watch her closely. Anne smiles drowsily at him. He seems kind. Gently his calloused hand lifts her blood-soaked hair and inspects the wound. A large gash extends from her parietal lobe to the base of her temple. Behind them, Evan is crawling closer.

He shouts, 'Go and get help! Please, go and get help!'

The old man does not react. With careful concentration, he reaches into his bag and takes out a used handkerchief. Again he lifts the damp hair and gently sponges the edges of the wound, the dirty cloth absorbing some of the blood. Anne closes her eyes and exhales heavily. The old man stills his hands, waiting for her breathing to settle. Ever so softly he parts the two lips of flesh. In the flayed skin, mixed in with the blood, are small white fragments: crushed splinters of the temporal bone.

Behind them, Evan finally drags himself up. Sweating, exhausted, his face stained with dust, he manages a final thrust of his hips and throws out his arm to catch the old man's ankle. The peasant jumps, startled.

'Sir . . . please . . . in the backpack, over there . . .'

Evan catches his breath and points to the wrecked motorbike.

'. . . A first-aid kit . . .'

The old man looks straight into Evan's eyes and gently shakes his head. He doesn't understand what he's saying. Panicking, Evan again points to the motorbike.

'Medicine . . . medicine . . .'

The old man glances at the bike and then turns to Evan and again shakes his head. In Tibetan he says, 'Your bike is smashed. There is nothing we can do with it.'

'Evan?'

Anne's voice is weak, quiet. Evan drags himself by his elbows towards her.

'Yes, Anne . . . I'm here.'

Anne attempts a smile.

'Evan . . . what's the time?'

Evan lowers his eyes and peers at the shattered face of his watch: 17.30.

'It's five-thirty.'

'No . . .' Anne has difficulty speaking. She shuts her eyes, opens her mouth and gasps for air. 'Not here . . . Back home.'

Evan clenches his fists to calm himself and makes a rapid calculation. 'Back home it's seven-thirty in the morning.'

With her eyelids shut, Anne smiles again.

'Lucy's eating breakfast.'

Evan carefully strokes her hair.

'Yes.'

The old man places his hand on Evan's shoulder and gestures for him to be quiet. Evan ignores him and turns back to Anne.

'I'm going to get the first-aid kit. I'll be right back. Okay?'

Anne hears his words in a jumble. Her eyes flutter open again. Her sight, too, has weakened. She blinks and squints wearily, trying to focus. No use. Evan remains a hazy smudge.

'Okay.'

'Okay, I'm going. I won't be long.'

The blurry face hanging over her moves and disappears. Anne has gone pale. Her breathing has become deep and heavy. The old man has noticed, but he keeps his distance, watching as Evan struggles over to the motorbyke, hauling himself through thorn bushes. Anne closes her eyes. The old man's eyes quickly flick over to check Evan's progress. He is now a fair distance away. The peasant removes his bag, places it on the ground, and kneels next to Anne, speaking soft Tibetan in her ear.

'You will die soon. I'm going to move you a little. Don't worry. It will do you good. It is to help liberate your consciousness.'

Anne knows she is being spoken to but cannot make out who is speaking nor understand his words. Her strength has gone. But politeness is ingrained in her, and so she digs into her reserves to answer with a benevolent blink. The old man acknowledges it with a sombre nod, rolls up the sleeves of his tunic and slips a hand under Anne's pelvis. She doesn't try to stop him. Her breathing accelerates. The peasant gently raises her hip and pivots her body onto her right side, in the same direction as her face on the stone. His movements are slow and delicate. Next he lifts her calves and brings her legs together, one on top of the other, moving her into a foetal position. Anne grimaces and moans softly. The old man stops and watches her. Gradually, Anne's face relaxes. Little by little, the pain ebbs away. Now he takes her left hand and places it flat on her left thigh, then takes her right hand and tucks it under her chin.

'There, it's done.'

He sits and turns around. Over by the motorbike, Evan scuffles about on his belly, rummaging through the scattered luggage. He is covered in dirt and bits of scrub; he looks like a small animal tirelessly rooting through the undergrowth. The old

41

man sighs, pulling some wooden prayer beads out of his pocket. He begins to chant.

'O Buddhas and Bodhisattvas,[6] O compassionate ones, this woman is about to leave this world and pass over to the other shore. She has not chosen to die. She has neither shelter nor anyone to help her. She is entering the darkness . . .'

Anne opens her mouth to breathe. Her lips are dry, her tongue sticky and swollen, her eyes still. A mirage appears to her: a thin layer of shimmering water slowly covering the ground, accompanied by the monotonous litany of the old man. The soft sound resonates in the background, woven into her vision.

'. . . She is falling into an abyss. She is entering a dark forest. She is beginning a great battle. O merciful ones, become her refuge. Guide her away from ignorance. Save her from the intermediate states. Help her cross the storms of *karma*. Do not let her drift towards inferior worlds. O merciful ones, use your compassion to help this woman . . .'

Through her open eyes, Anne can see nothing but her hallucinations. The water of the mirage slowly evaporates, rising from the surface of the earth in

---

[6] The Bodhisattvas are beings who, having themselves attained enlightenment, choose not to escape the cycle of rebirth in order to help all beings achieve enlightenment.

thick scrolls that billow up towards a crystalline sky. Anne shudders. The gaps between her abdomen's rise and fall lengthen. Her heart rate is slowing. The old man speeds up the flow of his words.

'. . . May compassion guide her when she is without energy, when she is separated from those who love her, when her friends can no longer support her and when she must wander alone. May she be conscious and free to choose her birth when she attends the union of her parents. For the good of others, may she obtain the best life to achieve her goals . . .'

The old man moves closer to Anne.

'Young woman, listen carefully. Your body has begun the process of dissolution. Everything must dissolve, even you. Earth dissolves into water, water dissolves into fire and fire dissolves into air. Understand that this reality is yours and have no fear. See the truth and accept it . . .'

Anne shivers from head to toe as if she were cold. She pants rapidly through her gaping mouth. A trickle of opalescent liquid drips from her nose, trailing down her cheek. Her jeans are wet with urine. The sound of the old man's voice loses its intensity and melts behind the cacophony of her own viscera, of the beating of her heart, the ebb and flow of blood in her arteries, the gurgling of her intestines. Her breathing grows ever more laboured. Her eyes wander, roll up into her head, return.

'May the sounds and lights you encounter not become your enemies. Those sounds are your sounds. Those lights are your lights . . .'

Behind wreaths of smoke, the mirage of the sky sinks into darkness and is replaced by a cascade of multicoloured lights. They flicker and dance, moving in the dark like a cloud of fireflies.

'. . . The *bardo* of the moment of death is upon you. Let go of all desires, all wishes and attachments. Accept leaving your body. It is made only of flesh and blood. It is ephemeral. Do not cling to illusions.'

A loud, hoarse shout interrupts the calm voice. The lights flash erratically, red, yellow, orange. They collide and merge, growing obscenely and bearing down on Anne.

Evan crawls desperately to Anne and the old man, dragging the first-aid kit behind him.

'What have you done? What have you done?'

Anne's stomach convulses. She hiccups. There is fear across her face. Evan stops level with the kneeling peasant, shouting roughly, 'Why did you move her?'

The old man urgently shakes his head, signalling him to lower his voice.

'Fuck off! Get lost!'

Evan pushes the old man hard, knocking him over. He leans towards Anne.

'Anne, I'm here. Don't worry. Everything's going to be all right.'

Anne's eyes have rolled back. Every breath she takes is interrupted by painful spasms in her diaphragm, followed by a lengthy exhalation. At her side, Evan struggles to open the first-aid kit. The zip is jammed. By tugging it up and down several times, he eventually manages to force an opening large enough to slip his hand inside. Hurriedly he empties out the contents: rolls of bandages, sticking plasters, scissors, packets of pills, a syringe, all of it soaked. Worried, Evan plunges his hand back into the bag, rummages at the bottom and cries out. He pulls his hand free, sucks his cut finger quickly, seizes the zip's two metal runners and tears them apart. The kit bag rips open. Inside, in a torn plastic pouch, are vials of medicine; all are smashed.

\* \* \*

The cavity is humid and dark, wrapped in a translucent, red-mottled membrane. There is no noise, not a sound.

At the peak of the chamber, a teardrop of blood forms. It grows, becomes round, distends under its own weight and detaches itself from the wall. The drop falls, peacefully, across the oblong pocket of flesh. At the bottom it explodes into a multitude of tiny pearls. They splash onto the glistening tissue, trickle down to the base and, like mercury, merge, into one. Against the stifled growl of a long, deep exhalation, the drop of blood regains its original shape, and is still.

A second drop of blood forms at the peak. It too detaches and slowly falls, dashing against the first drop. The beads born of the impact again roll towards the bottom and reunite in a new, larger drop at the sound of a second exhalation.

A third falls, bursts and blends with its two predecessors. They re-form into one, followed by the sound of a third exhalation, and then by silence. Nothing moves. The heart has stopped.

* * *

Night has fallen over the mountain. Evan is lit by a few flames. His hand, trailing on the ground, clutches the fragments of Anne's mobile phone. His face is wet with tears. He lies next to his partner. Anne is dead. Her eyes are open, her mouth gapes. Small, dark stains have appeared on her teeth. The lower part of her face, resting on the rock, is sticky with coagulated blood and the dried mucus that had leaked from her nose. Yet underneath these marks of suffering, her expression is peaceful. She looks calm.

On the other side of the fire, sitting cross-legged, the old man fingers his prayer beads and chants, gently rocking his body back and forth.

'Listen to me carefully. Do not allow yourself to be distracted. What we call death has now arrived. Soon you will see a bright light. In my country it is called the pure light. This light has no source; it is ageless. It comes from nothing and nowhere. Having neither beginning nor end, it cannot die . . .'

A strange glow spreads through Anne's corpse. Her clothes, her skin, her muscles and now her bones gradually lose their opacity and become transparent, revealing her internal organs. This transformation is visible neither to Evan nor to the old man.

'. . . This light has gone through many ordeals, but it is never affected by the evil it encounters. It has also encountered truth, but that does not change it either. It is in each of us, in every being and every place. Yet no one can see it. Look at it well. This light is the only reality. Concentrate. Emulate it: remain open, empty and pure. Recognise yourself in it and be liberated.'

A thick white substance collects in Anne's brain, then slowly spreads downwards. As it advances, it fills her with a whiteness that obliterates one organ after another. Another fluid, this one red, gathers in her uterus and rises towards her head, washing away her bladder, colon, small intestine, stomach, kidneys, liver. The two liquids meet at the level of her heart. On contact, they each become black. The darkness contaminates the body, moving outwards towards the corpse's extremities. Centimetre by centimetre, the body is erased, absorbed by the blackness until it disappears completely.

There is silence.

* * *

A halo appears in the gloom. Within the light hovers a slender silhouette: Anne. The light's intensity flares, flooding the space with a soft and intense clarity. Her nostrils dilate. She breathes in deeply, trying to absorb the moment, its smells and its quality. Her face brightens in amazement.

* * *

A bundle of dead wood tumbles loosely into the fire. The flames have died down now, the embers glowing on. The old man takes a branch and stirs them up.

On the other side of the fire, Evan shivers. He has

curled up with his back against Anne's corpse. He is awake with his mind elsewhere, his eyes focused on nothing. The old man walks around the fire and removes his tunic, kneeling beside Evan to cover him with it. He speaks in Tibetan.

'You should sleep a little. Tomorrow will be a long day.'

His gaze fixed in front of him, Evan shakes his head faintly and mutters in reply, 'Just leave me alone.'

The old man gets up, pleased to have exchanged a few words.

Anne is covered with the sleeping bag up to her shoulders, as if to protect her from the cold. Her skin has tightened, pulling out the wrinkles on her forehead and stretching the folds of her eyelids. The sun's first rays are reflected in the opaque veil that covers her corneas. Her swollen tongue fills her mouth. A purplish mark has appeared at the base of her neck. Despite death, her body is changing.

The peasant sits just above her head. He picks up a small branch, takes a knife out of his pocket and begins peeling off the bark while intoning.

'When the pure light appears, your spirit will be completely empty, liberated of its memories, its passions and desires. This light will fill you with joy. It is your original spirit. Like this light, your spirit knows neither birth nor death. Like this light, your spirit can conserve this emptiness, this joy. Understand it and concentrate. You have the chance to liberate yourself from suffering and to remain in peace. Recognise this –'

The old man breaks off. Out of the top of Anne's skull, a blurry, transparent discharge escapes, like the shimmer of heat above a radiator. Very still, the old man watches it intently. The vapour melts and dissipates slowly into the warm air, mingling with the orange tongues of the fire. The old man smiles.

'Noble one, your conscience has just left your body in the most auspicious manner. Now you will pursue your path towards liberation. There is no master beside you to help you and so I ask you to concentrate. Recall someone you have met in the course of your existence, a person whom you respected for their wisdom and goodness, a person in whom you had complete trust. Visualise this person. Consider him or her your master. Fill your heart and spirit with all that was best in that person and hear my words as if he or she were speaking them . . .'

# The Bardo of Reality

The foot of the mountain is submerged by the morning mist, which covers the valley like a ghostly veil. All is calm, silent, no one in sight. The area seems uninhabited, deserted.

Evan lies with his back to Anne. The grimy trails of tears dirty his face. He hasn't moved. He looks absently at the cooking pot set amid the embers: the steam rising from it, the string of a teabag hanging out.

The old man's calloused hand appears and taps Evan on the shoulder, making him jump and then grimace. The old man offers him a cup and whispers in Tibetan, 'Here, I've made you some tea.'

Evan turns around. Anne is still there, laid on her side, the sleeping bag placed over her. Flies have settled on her lips, at the entrance to her nostrils, on her clouded eyes. Evan swats them away. Unwinding his scarf from around his neck, he flattens it and lays it over her face. Motionless above him, the old man watches every gesture and waits patiently, holding the cup. Evan turns and scrutinises him in silence. Finally he makes up his mind, and takes the cup.

'Thank you.'

The old man answers with an affable smile. He lifts a finger to his lips to ask for quiet and returns to his place near the fire. Evan watches him warily, sipping his tea. The old man picks up several strips of trimmed wood, returns to him, crouches and speaks very softly.

'We must look after your leg.'

Evan doesn't react. The old man tries a second time to explain. He shows him the pieces of wood and places them about his calf, in the shape of a splint.

'Your leg. We have to treat it.'

Evan sniggers.

'What are you doing? You want to play at being a Boy Scout now?' He sighs miserably. 'Why didn't you go and find help?'

As though struck by a sudden pain, the old man wrinkles his eyes and flutters his hands in the air, making repeated gestures between his ear and Anne. Evan watches his gesticulations, stupefied.

'Oh no, don't tell me . . .'

The scarf over Anne's face flutters softly in the breeze.

'You don't think she can hear . . .'

Evan turns to the old man.

'. . . Do you?'

The old man lowers his head in confirmation and goes back to whispering.

'The sound of your voice can frighten her and

make her lose her way, especially if you shout or weep.'

Again he presents the splints to Evan.

'Not taking care of yourself will not help your wife.'

Evan observes the old man. Though he cannot understand his words, he can see the worry in his lined face. He sighs.

'Okay.'

Evan puts down his cup and inspects the ground around him. He bends and picks up two strips of gauze, then the scissors, and slips them into the pocket of the old man's tunic. He gathers up the packets of pills discarded in the dust and examines them. Choosing one, he extracts two pills and swallows them with some tea. The old man waits patiently, still kneeling on the hard ground before him. Evan holds out his hand to the old man, who takes it and helps him up. Evan points to a parasol pine about ten metres away and together they hobble over, before Evan slumps to the ground, whimpering with pain.

'All right? Are we far enough away? Can I talk now?'

The old man agrees without understanding, kneels and gives him the pieces of wood. Evan smiles at his persistence, takes the sticks and places them beside his fractured leg.

'You've got a nice face . . . It's a shame we have to meet like this.'

The old man grins kindly.

'You know you killed her, don't you?'

Evan looks him in the eye, impassive.

'Don't worry. I killed her too . . . I'm the one who wanted this trip . . . And we could just have slept up there last night.'

Evan lifts his eyes to the mountaintops, lost in thought. Struck by the first rays of the sun, the sky turns blue.

\* \* \*

In the shade, the back of his neck against the bark of the pine tree, his hips wedged between two roots, Evan fills his lungs with air. His face is covered with sweat and his eyes are closed. The damaged CD player lies against his chest. From the headphones on his ears seeps the hushed sound of the Bach presto that they had been listening to before the accident. His trouser leg is cut off at the knee and below it his leg is wrapped in bandages. The ends of the splints are poking out.

'Sir?'

Evan half-opens one eye. The old man is before him.

'Sir, can you hear me?'

The old man's indistinct voice blends with the violin. Evan presses the stop button. The old man smiles at him.

'Feeling better?'

Evan looks at the old man without reacting. Recognising the inanity of his question, the old man clears his throat and flutters his hand as if to erase it.

'My name is Tsepel.'

Evan still does not respond. The peasant taps his chest and repeats.

'Me, Tsepel. You?'

He points at Evan, who sighs.

'Evan.'

The old man nods uncertainly.

'Evan?'

Evan blinks in confirmation and weariness.

'Yes, Evan.'

The old man nods, stands up and launches into a speech.

'Evan, in a while I'm going to undress your wife and burn her belongings . . .'

Drained, Evan shuts his eyes, reopens them and listens stoically to the sounds of the old man.

'. . . She must understand that she no longer belongs to this world. She must accept that she has to leave her past life in order to be free. Do you understand?'

Evan is unresponsive. Tsepel speaks to him slowly and carefully.

'As long as she remains attached to her life, she will be unable to move from the immediate state . . .'

Evan turns his head towards Anne. The scarf that covered her face has been displaced by the wind. Her face is in full sunlight.

'. . . You mustn't be angry. You must stay calm. You must let her go. Otherwise, you will keep her here and increase her suffering. Act as if you were indifferent. Yes?'

Evan looks distractedly at the corpse. The old man gives him an affectionate smile.

'That's perfect.'

Tsepel searches in his pocket and takes out a strip of dried meat which he offers him.

'Here. You must eat. You need to get your strength back.'

Evan contemplates the withered curl of meat. He waves lazily to the things strewn around the remains of the motorbike.

'There's plenty to eat back there. Help yourself. I'm not hungry.'

He closes his eyes again.

* * *

The light is dwindling. A bird of prey circles in the

warm air. Evan opens his eyes, his back still against the tree, whose low shadow now stretches as far as Anne and covers her corpse with a sheet of coolness. At his post beside her, Tsepel continues his incantations.

'Yesterday you saw the pure light. If you did not recognise yourself in it, you are going to enter the *bardo* of reality and be wandering there . . .'

A vehicle horn sounds in the distance. Evan sits up abruptly and scans the mountainside. Tsepel grabs him out of the corner of his eye without halting his invocations.

'. . . When your spirit and your body separate, a bright force will appear to you. Its power is such that you may be frightened.'

The horn sounds again. Evan pulls himself out from the tree's roots and starts crawling towards the slope that leads to the road. The old man gets up and hurries to catch up with him. Just as Evan begins to clamber up the steep slope, Tsepel catches him fast by the foot. Evan turns. The sound of a large diesel engine echoes around the valley.

'There's a truck coming. Can't you hear it?'

'Calm yourself. No vehicle ever comes this way.'

Evan shakes his foot free and continues climbing. Wearily, the old man removes his spectacles, rubs his eyes, smooths his eyebrows and places the frame back against his nose.

'Wait!'

He catches up with Evan again, this time placing hands under his armpits and pulling him up the rocky slope. The engine sound is getting closer. The pebbles of the rough slope begin to slip under their feet, tumbling back down towards the ledge, but Evan will not be deterred. With renewed effort he hauls himself up against the shifting ground of the rockslide. Tsepel taps on his arm for attention.

'Look behind you.'

Evan ignores him and continues to climb. Tsepel grips him by the shoulders and turns him onto his back, like a tortoise. Evan struggles.

'Let me go!'

The old man points to the opposite side of the valley. Evan stops. Several kilometres away, glinting in the hot light of the sun, a golden dot advances slowly across the mountainside.

'No one ever comes this way. The road is too poor.'

Out of breath, gasping through his open mouth, Evan stares after the vehicle as it drives out of sight. The old man taps his thigh in consolation.

'We must take care of your wife. She's the one most in need. I'll get help for you later. Don't worry.'

\* \* \*

The sun has just set, and in the twilight the fire has been rebuilt. Tsepel brings over a new bundle of branches, dropping it on the pile already gathered. He rubs his hands clean and turns to look at Evan. With his back against the tree, head tipped to one side, he seems to be asleep. Tsepel walks towards him, stops before his long outstretched legs and watches him closely. Evan's eyes are closed. His breathing is deep and heavy.

'Evan?'

Evan doesn't move. Tsepel turns around and heads towards the wrecked motorbike. Step by step he picks his way through the dusk, inspecting the ground. Every now and again he stoops to pick up a scattered item: a dress, a bra, photographs, a box of tampons . . . Arms full, he returns to the fire and spills his harvest beside the dead body. Three times he goes back and forth, sorting through the spilled luggage and gleaning everything that can only belong to Anne. The task done, he returns to Evan's side and delicately replaces his tunic over the young man's torso. Troubled in his dreams, Evan lifts his head, snorting, but is still deep in sleep. His head slowly sinks back on his shoulder. He begins to snore.

Reassured, Tsepel goes back to the fire and kneels before Anne. He pulls back the sleeping bag covering her, bundling it up and leaving it to the side. He places his left hand on the top of her thorax, slips his right under her pelvis and pivots her body onto its back. Anne's head rolls on the rock, her neck stretching out. Her limbs flop to the side. One by one, Tsepel undoes the buttons of her torn shirt and opens it. The skin is dry like parchment. Her breasts slump outwards, along the line of her ribs. The pink blush of her nipples has faded to a pale grey. Her hips are dotted with purplish marks. A large green stain blotches her navel. Tsepel slips an arm under the corpse's neck and lifts the trunk. Anne's head falls against her collarbone. Tsepel catches the sleeves of her shirt and pulls. The white cotton slips over her back. He puts it aside and gently lays down the half-naked torso. He unbuttons the trousers, gets up and places himself level with the legs. Standing, he lifts the ankles one after the other, unties the laces of the shoes, takes them off and removes the socks, discarding them on the ground. He grips the hem of the jeans and tugs them off. Anne's flaccid belly sloughs with the movement. The thick material slips as far as the instep and comes away. Once released, the bare legs drop heavily to the ground. He leans forwards to take hold of the elastic of her panties. The thin piece of cotton rolls up and catches around her buttocks, eventually giving way under Tsepel's insistence. Anne, lying on her back, is completely naked.

Tsepel opens out the shirt and uses it to parcel up the other clothes and his haul gathered from the bike, roughly tying the sleeves together to secure it. He lifts the bundle and throws it into the fire. The shirt sleeves unravel and Anne's photographs slide into the fire. Lucy is eaten by the flames, puffing thick whorls of smoke which are carried by the wind over to the parasol pine. Evan coughs and splutters awake. The old man stands impassively in front of him, poking Anne's clothes into the fire. Immediately behind him, the naked remains of Evan's partner tremble in the heat haze. Evan roars.

'No!'

Forgetting his leg, he tries to stand up and promptly falls, screaming even louder. The old man dashes towards him, hugs him tightly and silences him by clapping his palms over his open mouth.

'Don't shout. You'll frighten her.'

Evan's appalled eyes are riveted on the corpse and he is overcome with nausea. A thick yellow liquid oozes out between the old man's clenched fingers and dribbles down Evan's chin. Tsepel lets go and plunges his vomit-soiled hand into his trouser pocket, pulling out a dog-eared photograph of the Dalai Lama and brandishing it before Evan's eyes. Bile dripping from his chin, Evan sobs in silence.

* * *

The stars glitter against the vault of the night sky. Tsepel is back beside the fire. He has taken to his prayers again.

'You are not the first one to leave this world. It happens to every one of us. Do not hold on to any desire or any wish for this life . . .'

To his left, Anne's corpse is covered again with the sleeping bag. Her waxy feet, placed neatly together, stick out from the bottom.

'. . . You can no longer stay here. Your only way is to continue until you find your path . . .'

Evan is also back in place, propped up against the pine. Carefully arranged around the two roots that prop him up are piles of freeze-dried meal packets, CDs, the remains of the first-aid kit and some clothes. On top of a woolly jumper the photograph of the Dalai Lama rests, secured by a pebble.

'. . . The visions that will appear to you may frighten you, but you must understand that they are not real. They are harmless. You will be frightened but safe, like a child who sees monsters in the shadows . . .'

Motionless under the tunic, Evan clasps one of the torn backpacks to his stomach. He smiles and stares vacantly into space.

'. . . Your visions are the fruit of your own projections, your imagination and memories. Everything you will see is merely the projection of your spirit.'

\* \* \*

There's a spark in the blackness. It expands and unfurls into a tight, shimmering marble, then a ball of light. As the light grows it gradually reveals at its centre a heart, motionless. The ball becomes a globe and continues to expand; as it swells outwards the interior becomes illuminated. First a breast is shown, then a hip, a belly, a navel. It is the body of a young woman. Her pallid, translucent skin looks silky, as though dusted with a thin layer of powder. Her flesh is firm, full and taut, her curves flawless, unmarked by wrinkles or imperfections. A chin appears, then red lips, two cheeks, a small beauty spot on the right one. Anne smiles.

'. . . Whatever the images you see, whatever sounds you hear, know that they cannot harm you. You cannot die . . .'

In one sudden movement the circumference springs out and the brightness of its interior intensifies, encircling and illuminating Anne in her entirety. Motionless, she floats, freed from gravity. Her eyes are wide open. In front of her, on the other side of the translucent sphere, she sees a sun born of the darkness, a dawn without a horizon. The day star rises out of the blackness. With unnatural clarity it illuminates a portion of infinity: an azure sky, a pearly lake, a large plain covered with amber wheat swaying in an emerald wind. Thunder rumbles in the distance.

'. . . These images and sounds reflect only yourself. Try to recognise yourself in them. Remember this and find peace.'

The vast landscape begins to turn in on itself, spinning faster and faster, and soon it is nothing more than a collection of multicoloured particles filling space. There are radiant beams of light that gravitate towards Anne, travelling across her body until they meet at her heart. Beating, the fist-sized pack of muscle reflects the beams outwards onto the inside surface of the sphere, coating it in a wash of primary colours that shift like the iridescence of a soap bubble. Slowly the colours blend, coalescing into lines, contours, shapes. Forms become identifiable: faces, objects, places. A cascade of images covers the interior wall of the sphere, like a jigsaw puzzle whose pieces have no defined edges. Anne sees the images flash by at great speed, melting into one another in a dazzling array. She watches her destiny unfold.

Her first vision: surrounded by the blinding halo of the operating lamp, the green-masked faces of the medical personnel, blurred and deformed by the residue of amniotic fluid left in her eyes.

Next, a bathroom of pale blue earthenware tiles. In the oval mirror above the porcelain sink, Anne sees herself for the first time, in her mother's arms. A young, resplendent Rose, with her cheek on her daughter's head, singing a lullaby and rocking her.

A clumsy little hand knocks over a glass baby bottle. The bottle rocks on the high chair tray and drops onto the grey tiles, smashing and spilling milk everywhere.

On the big, solid wood table sits a birthday cake, covered in white cream and sugared fruits. On the top, two pink-and-white-striped candles burn in tiny plastic crowns.

An enormous fluffy panda, wedged between colourful cushions on a brown velvet couch, pleads for a playmate with his hard, shallow eyes.

Weightless in the sphere, Anne is buffetted from side to side by the images. Her features slide from fear into laughter, from seriousness to tender recollection.

* * *

Five Vietnamese children flee, weeping, along a country road, followed by four armed soldiers. At the centre of the black-and-white photograph, there is a little girl of about ten, naked. Her arms are spread wide, her face disfigured with pain;

she advances, her mouth distorted with her silent scream.

Slumped across the kitchen Formica table, his head on his folded arms, her father, John, in his thirties, sobs.

Hector, a German pointer, leaps about desperately on a terrace of black slate beside the sea, trying to catch a little twitching fish held out by a laughing man in his sixties.

Ears to the wind, sending up a spray of saltwater droplets, Hector gallops along the water's edge, rejoicing in his freedom.

On the big screen, carried away by a waltz, Bambi spins on the ice, hooves splayed.

On the first day of school, the teacher shoos parents from the classroom. The children cry and bawl, Anne among them.

Rose is towering and furious. She raises her arm and brings it down fiercely. Six-year-old Anne, hand to her cheek, looks up with terror at her giant of a mother. The wallpaper behind is riddled with childish scribbles.

Anne's grandfather is laid out still and cold on his bed. He is dressed impeccably in a dark suit. His face is weirdly puffy, his skin pale and flabby.

A metal bowl on a tiled floor. Dog food strewn all around it.

Locked in her sphere, powerless, exposed to her past, Anne weeps.

A teenage Anne lies naked on her back, offering herself. A young man at the foot of the bed marvels at the sight of her.

The rain drives down on a dark night. Drenched to the bone, Anne zooms down an empty street on her bicycle, shrieking with joy.

Anne, wearing a hired gown, stands on a stage on a sportsfield to receive her high-school diploma.

Inside the sphere, Anne is euphoric.

\* \* \*

Lugging a large green portfolio, garishly dressed in hip clothing, Anne passes for the first time through the high wooden door of the New York Academy of Art.

The band at a crowded bar is playing the blues. Her hair tousled, Anne dances alone on the dance floor, watched lazily by amused patrons. A stranger, a man in his early forties, catches her by the arm, twirls her twice, rolls her along his arm and kisses her. Anne lets him.

The atmosphere is reverential. Anne poses naked for a group of students in a life painting class. A curly redhead gazes at her lovingly, his canvas blank.

Lying front-down on an unmade bed, her chin propped on her crossed hands, a naked Anne contemplates a pair of firm buttocks. With his back to her, stark naked in the disorderly kitchen, the redhead is making coffee.

An old red Oldsmobile Cutlass is parked in front of the house, wrapped in a huge sky-blue ribbon, a large number 23 painted in black on its hood. John, Rose and Anne stand in the doorway. Rose takes her hands from Anne's eyes. Anne jumps and shrieks, smothering her parents with excited kisses.

Dressed to the teeth, her hair tightly pulled back, Anne finishes writing her name on the blackboard and turns around. A classroom of teenagers stares back at her.

Anne, drunk, staggers down a street in the dead of night. A young man props her up and helps her climb the front steps of a 1920s apartment building.

Locked in the toilet, Anne is staring at a white plastic stick in her hands. There is a tiny window in the stem. Two parallel pink lines slowly appear.

The Mother Superior smilingly thanks Anne one last time on the school steps, then closes the door with firm finality.

A jumble of grey shapes on the ultrasound screen fuse and part like protozoa. Suddenly, clear forms coalesce: a fan of Lilliputian toes, a foot, two legs, two arms, a head. In the middle of the trunk, a tiny jellyfish contracts: the beating heart.

Drifting in her bubble, Anne smiles, her eyes wet.

\* \* \*

There is a black box like a coffin in the centre of the circus, directly beneath the peak of the big top. A midget clown disguised as a baby is wriggling on Anne's belly. Anne screams in pain; the audience shakes with laughter.

Rays of sunshine sneak through the closed blinds and glow against the wall. Henry is in bed. Anne, pregnant, sits beside him drawing.

A long, deserted beach is bathed in sunlight. Henry, on all fours, finishes covering Anne with sand. Submerged up to her neck, she throws back her head and laughs.

Henry, on his knees, draws the face of a little girl on Annie's prominent, pregnant belly with a marker pen. Troubled, standing bare-chested before him, Anne lets him.

Anne frowns inside the sphere.

\* \* \*

Anne, dressed in a nightgown, lies propped up

against a mountain of pillows. Through tired eyes, she gazes lovingly at the suckling newborn. Henry watches unseen from the corridor through the half-open door, not daring to enter.

A small provincial airport. On the asphalt, Anne walks towards the plane, a Moses basket in her arms. She stops and looks for Henry through the terminal windows. He isn't there.

Anne sticks a poster in the window of a pizzeria. Her name features under the copy of a batik print of a white wolf with open jaws.

The gallery of her first show is packed. On the walls hang batik prints of tutelary gods and one portrait of Henry. Gusts of laughter rise above the hubbub. In a corner of the room, Anne is holding a drink and talking enthusiastically.

Inside the sphere, Anne has lowered her head. Eyes closed, she sobs.

* * *

A hospital corridor at night. Soaked, in tears, her face streaked with blood, Anne stamps her feet hysterically while banging on the window of the resuscitation room.

Anne is running in Central Park in the rain, pushing a baby's pushchair down a tree-lined avenue. A young man shouts and catches up with them.

It's Evan, his face bright and enthusiastic, almost unrecognisable.

The familly kitchen is a mess. Evan is seated in front of the little girl, who is wearing a red helmet full of black holes, a ladybug. He feeds her. She silently spits the food out again. Anne and her mother laugh.

Anne has cut her hair. Sitting cross-legged on the Persian carpet in her parents' living-room, she leafs through a book on tangkas.[7] Leaning against the fireplace, Evan oberves her, smiling.

Anne sits on her rope bed by the side of the road, paralysed with fear. The truck starts up in the darkness. The lemon and the baby's shoe sway under menacing eyes.

The motorbike soars over the precipice. Anne turns silently against the white sky, her arms open in welcome.

Inside the sphere, Anne's eyes are closed. Serenely she relives the freedom of the long, still fall, the suspension of time. The old man's voice penetrates, a brutal interruption.

'Even if you have practised spirituality all your life, until you recognise these projections they will avail you nothing.'

---

[7] Buddhist or Hindu religious paintings or embroideries.

Anne opens her eyes. The whole of the inner surface of the sphere is covered with images of Lucy. She plays cheerfully in the bath tub, under the amused eyes of her grandparents. Her head is bandaged.

The Bardo of Rebirth

Dawn's first glimmers pick out the contours of the jagged, snow-capped peaks. Everywhere, as far as the eye can see, mountains at once menacing and indifferent envelop themselves in light and are reborn, almost as though this peaceful, near-divine progression were quite banal. Lost deep at the lowest point of this immensity winks a tiny glimpse of saffron. Trapped between the deep black of vegetation and the milky grey of rock, it endures, a tiny reassuring fire in the middle of nowhere. In front of it, imperturbable, Tsepel continues to stir up the embers while incanting.

'Even if you have studied the sacred texts for centuries, they will be of no use to you until you recognise your projections. If you do not recognise your projections, you will never know peace . . .'

Several metres behind him, Evan leans against the pine. He is shivering. Under the peasant's tunic he clasps the empty backpack to his stomach. His breathing is a series of long, steady, almost soothing sighs. His mind wanders, carried on wave after wave of evanescent memories: a cup of hot chocolate, the cafe in Central Park, Anne's laugh, the loose laces of her red trainers, the sunflower on Lucy's pushchair, the dark grain of damp pavement, the flaming maples of the fall, a rake gathering yellowed leaves . . . He no longer has the strength to focus on one image and pause the flow of time, but he refuses obstinately to fall asleep, to leave Anne alone with this madman. But there is more to it than that. He doesn't want to let himself drift into the respite of dreams, to allow himself to escape. He is guilty, and the guilty must suffer. What a stupid idea. What a wretched, morbid education – but how can he rid himself of it? How can he discard this absurd, intense guilt that achieves nothing but the deepening of his despair? With eyes half-closed, Evan stares at the sparks jumping into the sky. And yet, just a few metres in front of him, Anne has reappeared.

She's seated there calmly, smothered in the smoke billowing from the fire. Her torn and bloodied white shirt is now like new, glowing so white that it is almost dazzling. Her body, too, is made new; her wounds have disappeared, leaving no trace of the accident. Disorientated in this unfamiliar place, she is intrigued by the strange old man in front of her who rocks and chants beside the fire. In vain she tries to wave the smoke from her eyes.

'. . . You will wake up and ask yourself what is happening to you. Your conscience will manifest itself in a similar form to the one you had before . . .'

Anne doesn't realise the old man is speaking

78

Tibetan. She understands every word he says, but other questions form in her mind.

Who is this man? What's he doing here in the middle of the night? And what am I doing here? Where is this place?

But Anne doesn't dare interrupt him to ask. He seems to be carrying out some sort of ritual and she is afraid of disturbing him. She tries to concentrate.

Who is he talking to? And what's he talking about?

She is sitting on the sleeping bag stretched over her own corpse, but she has not seen it yet. She still doesn't know.

'. . . You will have a physical body, made of flesh and blood, identical to your memories. But it will be radiant and in the prime of life . . .'

What am I doing here?

At last she makes up her mind.

'Sir?'

She waits for a reply but the old man has not heard her. She addresses him again, louder this time.

'Sir?'

No reaction. He continues speaking as if he were deaf.

'. . . it will be what is called a mental body. It is created by your unconscious and it will carry you to where you must be reborn . . .'

Anne listens to him. A shiver runs down her spine, a grim premonition. She gives herself a shake.

What's going on? Something's not right. There's something wrong.

Again she tries to wave the smoke away, but it continues to wrap itself around her, as if she hadn't moved at all. She doesn't notice, too busy peering through the half-light, trying to make out the scene around her: bushes, trees, rocks, a resinous smell. Like an arrow pointing the way, a thin ray of sunlight tops a peak and glints off the chrome ridges of the motorbike, the front wheel crunched out of shape by the impact. Slowly the ray of light widens, revealing little by little the scene of the accident. Anne closes her eyes and takes a deep breath. She remembers. She doesn't want to see any more, but she cannot halt the tide of memories that now flood her mind. Determined, she reopens her eyes, ready to confront whatever will come. A dozen metres away, at the foot of the conifer, Evan is also assaulted by the dawn. His head droops on his shoulder. His eyelids flutter. Sleep will soon overpower his will. Anne rushes to him and kneels at his feet. She is stupefied to find his face stained with dust, his clothes torn, his wounds and the improvised splint bound to his leg.

'Evan, what happened?'

Evan doesn't answer. Anne reaches out to shake

him by the shoulder, but instead of brushing the thick material of Tsepel's tunic, her hand passes straight through without the least resistance. Anne jumps back, letting out a cry, tripping over her feet. Although he is several metres away, the old man's voice reaches her clearly.

'. . . Listen closely. Even if you were blind, deaf or lame when you were alive, now your eyes can see, your ears can hear and your legs will carry you . . .'

The old man continues his impassive monologue near the fire. Neither he nor Evan has even blinked. And yet she cried out.

They didn't hear me? They didn't see me?

She stands up and looks at her hands.

What's going on? It can't be!

She is still a few seconds, her eyes frozen on Evan, then an uncontrollable scream tears out of her.

'Evan, wake up!'

The silence that follows is more deafening than her shout. The old man continues.

'. . . All your senses are clear and flawless. This is a sign that you are dead and that you are wandering in the *bardo* of rebirth . . .'

'Dead?'

That word!

Panic-stricken, Anne leaps up and turns to Tsepel, shouting, 'No! I don't believe it! It's a mistake, it must be a mistake. And even if it isn't, I refuse. I refuse! You can't make me!'

No sooner has she spoken than she realises she has betrayed herself. Knowing her voice cannot be heard, she has cried out anyway, every useless sound confirming what the old man has said. She knows, then, what has happened to her. Why else would she have shouted, why this anger, this rebellion? But how could she accept the unacceptable? She brushes away the knowledge, tries to pull herself together, to keep believing.

Okay, so they can't hear me, they can't see me – all right. I can't communicate with them any more. Okay, let's just calm down. I'm in some kind of other realm, maybe a bad dream, but there's no way that means I'm . . . No. It doesn't prove a thing.

Her mind grapples for a logical explanation that might dispel this nightmare, that might comfort her with its cool implacability. But it's impossible to hide from her hypocrisy. Why doesn't she dare say that simple word? Why shy away from using this inoffensive group of letters? Fear, fear is distorting her reasoning.

Stop. You've got to stop over-analysing, it's only making you more confused. Just believe it. Believe it! Even if it means believing a lie! You need to believe, so you can survive and fight!

God, what am I saying? Shut up. Shut up! Keep calm.

Anne sits down, shuts her eyes and slaps her head in frustration. She breathes in and out deeply several times to regain control of her thoughts. After ten seconds or so, she reopens her eyes.

Right, that's better. Let's start again. That word doesn't exist. As long as it doesn't exist, there's still some hope, the hope of waking up. What I need is a nice loud alarm clock, a bell so loud and piercing it could wake anyone from anything. Okay, several times all together, from all the mornings I have left to live. Come on, ring. Ring!

Anne turns to Evan. His eyelids remain closed.

'Evan, I'm begging you, answer me. It's not true what that man's saying. Tell me you can hear me. Evan, I'm begging you.'

She tries again to reach out and shake him but her hands pass through him without either of them feeling a thing.

'. . . Your body will be able to move without hindrance. You can walk through walls, houses, the earth, even Mount Kailash.[8] You can pass

---

[8] Tibet's highest summit, the source of the Ganges, Brahmaputra, Indus and Sutlej rivers, Kailash is considered the centre of the universe not only by Buddhists but also by Hindus and Jains, who call it Mount Meru.

through everything except for your mother's womb.'

Anne sits down, closes her eyes, covers her ears with both hands and pleads, 'Ring! Ring!'

\* \* \*

A clock ticks loudly in the night, keeping time as the shadows of trees dance against the ceiling. Outside, a light breeze sways the branches of a majestic lilac spangled with the orange glow of street lights. The room is filled with the sweet smell of the flowers. Anne's nostrils quiver. She slowly peels her hands from her ears and opens her eyes, her heart beating wildly. Before her stands the sink from her childhood. On the shelf above it, between a bottle of scent and a glass holding a small toothbrush and a tube of strawberry toothpaste, sits a big brass alarm clock.

Oh no. What now?

The clock's heavy tick had been the menace of her childhood insomnia, clunking through years of lost sleep. Anne quickly shakes her head to dismiss the useless memory. She wants neither to think nor to remember. She looks down. She is sitting on a bedspread printed with a pattern of different-coloured kites, the one from her bed at her parents' house. Anne turns her head. Lucy is lying bare-chested beside her. Her blonde hair sprouts out from the circular bandage around her head. The edges are wet with perspiration. It must be hot; yet Anne feels nothing. She bends over her daughter.

'Lucy?'

There is no reaction.

'Lucy!'

Lucy sleeps peacefully.

'Can't you hear me either?'

The little girl's chest rises and falls in a fluid, regular motion. Her skin glows like satin under the street lights, covered by a thin film of sweat. Anne watches her.

'Lucy, can you hear me? Oh, God, what's the point of my being here?'

With the back of her hand, Anne sketches a caress on her daughter's cheek.

'Lucy . . .'

Anne tries to hold back her sobs. She doesn't want to disturb her daughter.

'Lucy, I think I'm – dead . . .'

Anne tightens her lips and swallows her pain. Silent tears slide down her cheeks.

'Lucy, I need to talk to you.'

A tear drops onto the coverlet and vanishes.

'You're going to suffer because of me.'

Anne lies down, curled up against her

daughter, smelling her scent, stroking her face. Lucy turns over in bed, rubbing her nose. Her little face merges with her mother's while their fingers fuse. Despite her tears, Anne half-smiles.

'Well, there's one nice thing at least.'

She sits up gently and places a kiss on her daughter's temple.

'Do you feel anything?'

Lucy doesn't react. Anne lies back down beside her, closes her eyes and sniffs.

'You smell so good.'

\* \* \*

Sunbathers lie stretched out on their towels on the thin strip of white sand that cradles the sea. People stroll along the shore, keeping a watchful eye on the children playing in the waves. The sky is a deep blue, the weather perfect.

A little girl of about six wearing a bathing costume lifts her face from the thick hair of an old man. She is perched on his shoulders. Her long hair is tied with a pale green ribbon. She has a beauty spot on her cheek. The old man carrying the young Anne scrutinises the dunes.

'Can you see him?'

Anne leans roughly over the man's shoulder to look in his face.

'Grandpa?'

'Yes, Anne.'

She leans over some more.

'Grandpa, is it really you?'

She loses her balance.

'Hey, watch out!'

The man catches her by the knees, hoists her back on his shoulders and resettles her against the nape of his neck.

'Of course it's me. Who else could it be?'

'And you can hear me!'

Anne hugs her grandfather's neck.

'Easy now, you're strangling me!'

Anne lets out a long sigh of relief.

'Oh, I'm so glad you can hear me.'

Her grandfather lifts his hand.

'Ah, there he is at last!'

A German pointer with a liver and white coat comes running towards them out of the sun. Dazzled, Anne screws up her eyes and shields them with her hand.

'It's Hector!'

'Of course it's Hector.'

Her grandfather swings Anne off his back and kneels in front of her. He takes her by the shoulders and looks into her eyes.

'You feeling all right, Anne?'

Anne stares into his eyes for a moment.

'Yes . . . I'm fine.'

She catches his wrists and presses them tightly to her heart. He frees a hand and quickly presses his palm against her forehead to check for fever. Anne smiles at him.

'Don't worry. I'm fine. I'm just so happy to be with you, that's all.'

The dog joins them with a stick in its mouth and drops it at Anne's feet, retreating a little way. He looks at them with anticipation. Her grandfather picks up the stick and throws it. Hector scampers off.

Anne and her grandfather watch him go.

'He'll come back, won't he, Grandpa?'

The old man looks at her worriedly, then unfolds a sunhat from his pocket, placing it on her head and patting it gently.

'Of course he'll come back. What's the matter, my darling? You're asking some funny questions, talking oddly . . . Is anything wrong?'

'Are you dead too?'

Her grandfather flinches, knitting his brows.

'Now, do I look dead to you?'

'No. What about me? Do I look dead?'

* * *

The sunlight glitters on the water's surface. Waves lap gently against the old white hull as two little feet splash in the wavelets. Anne is sitting on the wooden deck, her shoulders framed between the forestay and the mast.

'Look!'

Her grandfather is standing in the stern of the sailing boat, with his back to her and the tiller held between his legs. His fishing rod is bent nearly in two. He's pulling in his reel as fast as he can, Hector leaping at his feet.

'It's a big one!'

Anne untangles herself from her rope harness and struggles to stand up as the boat pitches to one side. Thrown off balance, her grandfather sits down with a bump, still reeling in the line. A magnificent sea bass is pulled to the surface. It leaps and dives, frantically trying to free itself. Her grandfather drops the rod into the bottom of the boat, catching the nylon line, and hauls the fish up as Hector yaps at his feet. Catching the sea bass under its gills, Grandpa smoothly flicks out the hook. Impressed, Anne catches hold of the mast. Proudly he lifts his trophy. His features look drawn and his skin dull.

'Handsome, isn't he?'

Anne smiles admiringly, her hair whipping in the wind. The fish, with a muscular wriggle, slips from her grandfather's grasp and escapes back into the water, Hector leaping in after it. Anne bursts out laughing. Her grandfather, vexed, calls him back sternly.

'Hector, here!'

The dog swims in giddy circles, his expression contrite. Anne laughs uproariously. Her grandfather watches her, amused.

\* \* \*

The curtains are drawn in Anne's childhood bedroom, plunging the room into darkness. Anne is lying in her bed. Impassively she listens to her parents in the next room. Rose is sobbing.

'But why didn't he call us? Why didn't he say anything?'

John replies in a low voice.

'I don't know . . . Maybe because we live too far away? Maybe he just wanted to spare us any trouble . . . You know how he can be . . .'

Rose sniggers and sniffs.

'Spare us trouble? If you believe that you'll believe anything. That man is selfish to his core. He's been emotionally blackmailing me for thirty years. The bastard. Don't kid yourself he isn't loving every minute.'

Anne turns over abruptly in bed and buries her head under her pillow.

\* \* \*

A lizard disappears into the splendid wisteria that wreathes an old stone wall. Clusters of its violet flowers frame the French windows flung wide open onto a slate terrace. Anne is sleeping on a rattan lounger, a book open at her feet. Hector, his tongue lolling, patiently watches the line of ants triumphantly carry biscuit crumbs past his nose.

In front of the house the setting sun is slipping into the sea. All is calm. Anne's grandfather appears from behind a flowering hydrangea. He is wearing gardener's overalls and a straw hat on his head. A pair of secateurs sticks out of his pocket. He walks with painful slowness up the few steps that divide the garden from the terrace, pulling off his leather gloves at the top. His face is pale. He walks over to Anne and delicately parts the long hair that covers her face to kiss her forehead before picking up her book. He closes it and glances at the cover: *The Adventures of Ulysses*. He smiles, puts the book down, lifts Anne in his arms and disappears with her into the house. Hector trots silently after them.

\* \* \*

John, in his forties, is wearing a dark suit. He stands with his hands folded in front of his jacket, staring ahead. Rose is beside him, dressed in black. Her eyes are red above deep grey bags. Anne buries her face in her mother's skirt. Her lavender dress is a bright contrast with the sombre atmosphere. A seagull wails overhead. John raises his eyes and watches the bird disappear into the gathering clouds.

'We have to go. It's about to rain.'

Rose tries gently to free herself from her daughter, who instinctively tightens her grip around her waist.

'Come on, Anne, we have to go. It's all finished.'

The little girl ignores her.

'Darling, we need to go. Hector's waiting for us at home.'

Rose strokes her hair and looks pleadingly at her husband.

'Your mother's right, Anne. He's been locked up on his own for too long. We have to take him out. Remember, you promised to look after him.'

Anne slowly loosens her hold. John takes her hand, and together they turn and walk in silence away from the open grave behind them. Inside, on the coffin, lie a bouquet of daisies and a child's drawing of a little boat, full-sailed, adrift on a blue wax sea.

* * *

The wallpaper in the entrance hall is covered with dahlias, fuchsias and irises, in orange, faded pink and light blue. The cream-coloured front door opens. Anne walks cheerfully into the house, wearing her red duffel coat and swinging her black leather satchel.

'Hector!'

Anne slips the satchel off her shoulders and unbuttons her coat, revealing a thick Norwegian sweater. She stops and listens, motionless a moment. The lack of a response surprises her. She frowns.

'Hector?'

Still no answer. She takes off her coat, throwing it carelessly on the stairs, and crosses the hall to the kitchen door. Her foot kicks into Hector's bowl, spilling dog biscuits all over the stoneware tiles. Hector has eaten nothing. Anne gets annoyed.

'Hector!'

She spins on her heel and hurries into the living room through an adjoining door. Her footsteps echo through the house. She reappears in the hall and angrily climbs the stairs two steps at a time, treading over her coat.

'Hector!'

Upstairs her footsteps go faster and faster. Doors bang as she hurries from room to room. She hurtles back downstairs, rushes to the front door, flings it open and starts yelling, panic-stricken.

'Hector! Hector!'

She looks in every direction, waiting for a response. A soft voice startles her.

'Anne, stop shouting.'

Anne turns around. A laundry basket in her arms, her mother closes the door to the cellar and goes to her quietly.

'Mom, Hector's gone!'

Rose puts the basket down, takes her daughter's shoulders, pulls her close and presses her head to her stomach.

'I know.'

Paralysed, Anne stares in front of her. The wallpaper flowers begin to spin, faster and faster, pulling in the ceiling and dragging up the ground until suddenly all is darkness.

\* \* \*

In the little garden in front of the Victorian house Anne is helping her mother tamp down the soil around the sapling they've just planted.

'There, I think that'll do.'

Rose takes off her gloves and rubs her hands together.

'I'm sure he'll be comfortable here.'

Crouching on the grass, Anne continues to pat the soil with her bare hands, sniffling all the while. Her cheeks are covered in mud, streaked with tears. Rose gets up, steps back a little and admires her handiwork.

'He'll give us a beautiful lilac tree with lots of flowers. That way, we'll always remember him.'

Anne, in her white shirt, watches them from the brick wall behind them, pinioned by remembered grief. Her dirt-spattered cheeks are tear-stained, like those of the little girl she used to be. A bolt of blinding light strikes, propelling her back through the wall into the house. Carried away like a sailing boat loosened from its moorings, she is driven across the living room, through the hall, past the cellar door and down into darkness.

\* \* \*

Anne jerks upright, gasping for breath. Her face is slick with tears. She is sitting on a carpet of pine needles under Evan's tree, her knuckles white from her grip on the roots. It is broad daylight.

The stack of dead wood near the fire has grown. Tsepel pulls a steaming pot from the embers and carefully pours boiling water into a sachet of freeze-dried food. Anne lowers her eyes. On the ground, at her feet, lies the old man's tunic. Batteries, probably dead, have rolled into the filthy creases of the collar. Evan sits beside her, back against the trunk, headphones over his ears. On the CD player he listens with vacant eyes to the same Bach presto movement over and over again. Anne takes a deep breath, sniffs and tries once more to speak to him.

'Evan, you've got to help me out of this nightmare.'

He is unresponsive.

'Come on, Evan, just try. Speak to me softly. Say something, anything, but say something. I'll go crazy if I stay like this.'

Anne whispers in his ear.

'Evan, I'm begging you. I have to talk to you. Please try to make an effort. I need your help.'

Evan doesn't answer. Anne waves her hand in front of his eyes and whispers again.

'Evan, look at me.'

He doesn't flinch.

Shit, shit, shit.

The peasant approaches and hands the freeze-dried food to Evan.

'Sir!'

Evan takes the sachet.

'Thank you.'

The peasant nods his head gravely and turns around. Anne sticks out her leg to trip him. The peasant's ankle goes right through her calf. He shambles away in silence. He noticed nothing, felt nothing. Anne puts her head in her hands.

I've got to wake up. I've got to wake up.

She exhales deeply and wipes her eyes.

Okay. There's got to be a rational explanation for all this. Either that, or I've gone completely insane.

She inspects her surroundings again. She goes over to the discarded luggage strewn around the wrecked motorbike. A box of soap, their spare cash, her emptied toilet bag, plane tickets, a section of the map of India, a solitary flip-flop . . . Among Evan's clothes she notices the corner of a photograph. As she leans down to pick it up, she glances quickly at the old man and suddenly freezes, puzzled by the sleeping bag behind him. It's spread out on the ground, but the surface is lumpy and heaped up, as if it's covering something.

I hope that's not what I think it is.

Anne straightens up and treads carefully towards it.

It's not possible. It's not possible. Maybe it's wood, or maybe some sleeping stranger whose arrival I didn't notice . . .

Anne kneels in front of the sleeping bag and takes a deep breath, before trying to grab one end. The synthetic cloth does not move but becomes transparent, transformed by her touch. She sees feet, white, bloodless.

Screaming, she jerks backwards as the transparency scuttles up the rest of the sleeping bag. A whimper escapes her. She cannot take her eyes away from her own decomposing corpse.

The lifeless skin, now grey, is covered in fine wrinkles. Her left cheek is streaked with brown lines that stretch from nose to earlobe. A large, dark stain covers half her neck. Her eyes have caved into their sockets, sunken behind a milky film. Between her silvery lips, the buds on her swollen tongue are granulating.

Anne's breath escapes her. Her carotid artery hammers in her neck. Blue swollen veins stand out in her forehead. She doubles over, crossing her arms to compress her abdomen, then stiffens suddenly and groans to the sky.

\* \* \*

The sun is at its highest point. Apart from a few mean, slender shadows cast by the trees, there is nowhere to shelter from the crushing heat.

Tsepel has stripped. Standing in just a vest, a dirty rag on his head, he is soaked in sweat, which drops past his eyelashes into the white of his eye, stinging. He rubs his eyelid and continues with his incantations.

'With your new form, you will be able to see your house, your parents and those dear to you. You will want to speak to them but they will not hear you . . .'

Sitting by a thorn bush a few steps away, Anne contemplates her corpse. In the sun her white shirt is more dazzling than ever. Neither the heat nor the thorns sticking through her jeans have any effect on her. Her tear-stained face is totally expressionless.

'. . . Then you will feel a pain like that of a fish cast up on the sand under a blazing sun. This suffering no longer has any reason to exist. Even if you are attached to your loved ones, you are no longer with them. Detach yourself and avoid suffering . . .'

Anne shuts her eyes and sings through a humourless grin, 'Ring-a-ring o' roses, a pocket full of posies, a-tishoo, a-tishoo, we all fall down.'

'. . . You will possess supernatural powers resulting from your *karma*. You could go around the world in a fraction of a second . . .'

A solitary cloud passes in front of the sun. The peasant lifts his eyes and wipes his forehead. Drunk with shock, Anne continues impervious.

'Humpty Dumpty sat on a wall, Humpty Dumpty had a great fall . . .'

'. . . Your thoughts will take you instantly wherever you wish to go. You can visit any place at any time. But if you can avoid using your powers, do so, for they will not help you . . .'

'Anne?'

Now I'm hearing my own voice . . .

The voice calls out again, closer and more sternly.

'Anne!'

Anne sighs, turns her head wearily and opens her eyes. There is no one there.

Thought so.

'. . . These powers simply mean that you are in the *bardo* of rebirth. The important thing is to realise that you can make anything you want appear before you . . .'

Anne looks all around her. Tsepel and Evan have not left their posts.

'Anne, what have you done with your life?'

Startled by the proximity of the voice, Anne twists around. In front of her, sitting on her corpse, is her double. It wears a black robe lined with white fur, a stiff wing collar with white bands, and a long rolled wig that pours down onto its shoulders. Anne looks at her double, astounded. It stares back at her. Under Anne's gaze its pupils seem to begin to dilate, expanding further and further outwards like a mammoth monstrosity. The crystalline lens warps and thickens round the curve of the eyeball, angling the rays of light as they sink ever deeper into the vitreous body. Deep into the eye, far back, on the retina, the light rays are imprinted on darkness, and Anne can clearly distinguish her own tiny inverted image. She shakes her head, trying to break her gaze, but she is caught. She sees her reflection grow as it mirrors her movements, expanding massively as Anne is pulled closer and closer towards the eye, through the cornea and diving into the aqueous humour. She is flipped through the lens and dragged into the eye's dark interior, sinking further and further in. As she draws close her reflection seems to develop an independence, holding still, confident, superior, insolent. Now face to face with her image, each the same size, Anne brings up her arms in an ineffectual defence. She begins to scream, as her outstretched fingers reach her reflection and disappear one after the other inside it, followed by her palms, her wrists, her forearms, elbows, shoulders. Centimetre by centimetre, her body is consumed. Once the last toenail is devoured the reflection inhales deeply. The blackness around it begins to convulse, sucked into a vortex and swallowed into the reflection's mouth until all that is left is a bottomless, horizonless void. Swollen lungs near bursting now exhale. A blinding light escapes from the mouth. It overwhelms the emptiness, eclipsing the reflection until it itself is swallowed up completely.

* * *

On the television in a dimly lit room a journalist is reading the news. The sound is strange, tinnily distorted as though reverberating against the inner walls of the television.

101

John is sitting up in bed in his pyjamas, looking through some paperwork on his knees. The window is open a crack, the net curtain stirring slightly in the breeze. The door beside the dresser opens as, Rose steps out of the bathroom, turning off the light and coming back to the double bed. At the back of the room, pressed up against the sand-coloured wallpaper, Anne watches. Rose takes off her dressing gown, folds it in half and places it neatly on a chair.

'Mom?'

Mom, please, answer me.

Rose doesn't respond. She slips under the sheets and pulls them over her stomach. Anne calls out to her again, more loudly, 'Mom!'

Rose turns to the night table, takes the remote control and turns off the television.

What am I doing here? What's the point of all this?

'Mom, I need your help!'

Rose turns out the light and sinks her head into the pillow.

'John, turn off the light, will you?'

'I just need to finish this report I have to present at the meeting tomorrow. I won't be long. Did you check on Lucy?'

'Yes. She's sleeping like an angel.'

Anne goes and sits on the edge of the bed near her mother. Rose yawns and shuts her eyes.

What on earth am I doing here?

Anne studies the room carefully. The dresser mirror catches her attention. Rather than reflecting the room, it seems to radiate a strange light as though lit from within. Intrigued, Anne gets up and goes over to it. In the mirror, surrounded by a blinding halo, her reflection calmly examines her. It wears the black judge's robe. Anne lowers her head and stares uncomprehendingly at her jeans and white shirt.

'Don't you think it's time to take a look at your life?'

Suddenly the presto from Bach's violin sonata throbs into the room. Anne covers her ears and screams, 'Leave me alone!'

* * *

An engine backfire barks against the din of the sonata. Hands pressed against her ears, Anne turns round and round, trying to find something to latch on to, screaming.

She is on the mountain track, at the spot where they left the road. Dumbfounded, Anne keeps her eyes fixed on an amber cloud of dust rising into the sky. A few bends away, the Enfield is speeding towards her.

Anne is sitting dreamily on the back of the bike, her head on Evan's shoulder. He is concentrating, carefully calculating the dangers of the road ahead. Anne sits up. A flash of common sense lights up her mind.

We have to stop the bike.

Anne tries to raise her arm to tap Evan's shoulder but it won't move. None of her limbs will respond. She tries to say something but the words stick in her throat. Anne starts to sob, but nothing appears on her face, not a frown, not a tear. She feels a tingling in her legs, the jolts of her head bouncing on Evan's shoulder. She can feel the coolness of the breeze on her skin, can smell the vegetation and feel the sun's dazzle, yet she can neither move nor speak. She is locked in a body that belongs to the immutable past. She's crying inside. Evan cannot see it.

Why all this torture? Why won't it stop?

Her eyes see the landscape transformed by speed, forms and shapes melting into abstract lines, multicoloured and shimmering.

A few hundred metres on, the motorbike disappears around a bend. Anne is standing on the path again. Sharp and regular crunching noises, like footsteps on gravel, blend with the pulse of violins. They're coming from behind. Anne turns around. Drowned out by the din, Tsepel is walking calmly down the middle of the track. The motorbike speeds round the bend. Anne starts to shout.

'Stop! Stop! Evan, stop the bike!'

She knows that Evan cannot see her. She knows that he cannot hear. Yet she cannot help desperately waving her arms to warn him. It makes no difference. The motorbike continues on its path and swerves into the last bend.

I can't give up, I can't give up.

Anne turns around and rushes to the old man.

'Go away! Get out of the way!'

She tries to push him to the side, but first her hands, then her body pass straight through him.

The motorbike emerges from the last bend. The sun's blinding light glints off the chrome surface of the headlight. Evan sits up and stiffens on the bike. His foot presses down hard on the brake. The wheels lock. Stones fly.

\* \* \*

Anne is screaming in panicked terror. She sits beside her corpse, blinded by the sun. The Bach thunders on, slicing the air with its high-pitched staccatos. The old man appears beside the corpse; stooping, he rips the headphones off again. Abruptly the music stops. Gasping, Anne crawls backwards on her forearms. The old man grabs Evan under the

105

armpits, lifts him and drags him away from the body. Evan tries to wriggle out of his grasp.

'Get off me! Leave me alone!'

Anne watches the scene, petrified. Tsepel drops Evan back under his tree and, for the first time, raises his voice.

'Why did you put the headphones on her head? I told you not to disturb her! No music, no caresses, no talking, no tears – nothing! It will only increase her suffering. She's dead! You must accept it. If you cannot, at least try not to make her suffer through your own selfishness.'

*Selfish.* Tsepel repeats the word several times in his head as he marches back to the corpse. He pulls the sleeping bag back over Anne's face, sits down in front of the fire and resumes his prayers. His voice trembles. His right foot, which is crossed over his left thigh in a prayer position, shakes nervously. He has lost his calm.

'Young woman, you must listen carefully! Whatever the projections you are currently seeing, do not follow them . . .'

Anne listens to him, crying.

'. . . Do not let yourself be drawn in by your projections. If you let them carry you away, you risk losing yourself and you will worsen your pain.'

Anne turns her head towards the parasol pine. Evan has disappeared. She cranes her head to see past the tree. A few metres further up, Evan is trying to climb out of the ravine, clutching at the exposed roots. Anne jumps to her feet at once and runs to catch up with him.

'Evan, wait.'

Evan stops suddenly and turns around, dripping with sweat. Below, the old man has seen him but averts his eyes.

Tsepel sighs. He has decided not to budge. Evan must take care of himself. No one can do his mourning for him, and as long as he refuses to accept the situation, he will not manage. How hard it is to listen when we are burdened with the illusion of control, the conviction of knowledge. How to explain it to him?

For the first time, Tsepel re-evaluates his own actions. It is clear Evan understands neither his gestures nor his intentions. Westerners have their own gods, their own beliefs, their own rituals. What right has he to impose his? Ought he merely to find help and leave them alone? Does compassion justify prescribing what one thinks is best? Or could it be guilt that's keeping him here, the confused feeling that mixes moral duty and responsibility? Selfish – who's the selfish one? Tsepel stops praying.

Evan looks up and realises how far he has to climb and how steep the slope is.

'Evan, stop. You can't go anywhere with your leg.'

Anne slumps beside him.

'Come on, come back down.'

Evan looks afresh at the old man at the foot of the ravine, beside his partner. He appears defeated. Should he leave him alone? Evan, in turn, begins to analyse the purpose of his own actions. Should he go? Where? And why? None of this makes any sense to him. If he leaves, he would be abandoning Anne instead of staying by her side and trying to protect her. And, if Tsepel's prayers are helpful to Anne, there's everything to gain. If they are not, there's nothing to lose. Either way, Anne is still dead.

'You're right, Evan. Don't leave me alone. I still need you.'

Anne has heard everything. Hearing Evan's thoughts feels natural to her; in life she had always believed she could read her loved ones' thoughts.

Evan lets himself slide back down the slope.

'Don't worry, Evan. Everything will be fine.'

Anne strokes his hair affectionately. Her hand disappears into the tangled mass.

'Don't you think it's time to take a look at your life?'

Anne turns swiftly to find the source of the voice. But apart from the old man beside the body, the rocky ledge is deserted. Anne chews her cheek in worry. On her head sits the grey wig. In place of her shirt, a black silk robe with a white wing collar and bands. Anne has noticed nothing. But she, now, is the lady of the law.

* * *

Heartbeat, arterial pressure, breathing rate, oxygen levels – some lines undulate, some sharply pulse. Numbers blink on the screens, bleeping. In the all-white room, the medical personnel are hunched over the milky body of a baby laid out on a turquoise sheet. Two electrodes are stuck to its chest. The nurses stand back and the paddles discharge. The little body stiffens and jumps on the table. The infant's blonde hair is matted in clumps, stained with blood. Its delicate eyelids flutter. Lucy, her face deformed by bruises, unrecognisable, starts to breathe again.

Pressed against the window of the resuscitation room, Anne, in tears, bangs her fists on the glass. Her face, too, is bloodied.

Henry appears at the end of the corridor. He's limping. He has a plaster over the ridge of his left eye and his arm is in a sling. He stops short at the sight of Anne. Ten metres away, he stands waiting, perfectly still. Anne turns her head and glowers at him. Henry is motionless, accepting her gaze. Anne looks away furiously. In the resuscitation room, Lucy's pulse is steadying. Henry starts limping forward again, cautiously. Anne ignores him, staring ahead as she grits her teeth and swallows. Henry stops in front of the window. They stand side by side, eyes fixed on Lucy's prone figure. The tension between them is taut and ugly. Henry tries to bridge the gap.

'How is she?'

Eyes black with hatred Anne turns to him slowly. He shakes his head imploringly.

'I'm sorry. I didn't want this.'

Anne lifts a trembling hand towards the ceiling.

\* \* \*

The embers breathe, now red with life, now blackened with fatigue. Day dawns wearily. The old man prays beside the fire.

'As in a dream, you will not be able to control either your travels or your encounters. You spirit will be blown about like a feather in the wind . . .'

On the other side of the fire, Anne sits huddled on her corpse, her arms protectively bracing her head.

'. . . Death will question you about your life. It

will frighten you terribly and you will lie to it, pretending that you did no harm. So it will look you straight in the eye and, like mirrors, your eyes will reflect the whole of your life . . .'

Tsepel stirs the fire. His voice alters, becoming higher and more gentle. Clouds of sparks fly up. Anne is eclipsed behind them.

'. . . All your virtuous actions will be shown clearly, but also all your faults . . .'

Tsepel's voice has started to sound more like Anne's, trembling, as though the sound were travelling along a pipe. A last burst of sparks crackles into the darkness. Anne can be seen again, lying beside the fire.

'. . . Death will drag you then by a rope around your neck. It will decapitate you, eviscerate you, tear out your heart, drink your blood, suck your brain and gnaw your flesh to the bone . . .'

Anne sits up suddenly and shakes her head, trying to concentrate on the voice. Her judge's robe has vanished. Tsepel prays calmly beside the fire. His voice has returned to normal.

'. . . Do not fear the punishments it inflicts upon you. You are already dead and cannot die again, not even if you are cut into a thousand pieces. You are emptiness. Everything you see is equally empty by its very nature. And emptiness cannot harm emptiness . . .'

Anne watches the old man closely. She listens to him.

'. . . They are merely projections born of your own confusion.'

\* \* \*

The wet paving stones of the footpath are lined with daffodils. Anne and Henry are on the steps, waiting outside the door to the house. Their differences in age and character are starkly obvious. Lively, her hair tousled, Anne is wearing bright red boots, rainbow-striped woollen tights and a large, bright polyester raincoat that bulgies over the maternal roundness of her belly. Henry stands straight as a poker, his greying hair carefully coiffed. His slate-grey three-piece suit is smartly tailored in a severe style. His expression is tense. The door before them opens; Rose, smiling, is also wearing her Sunday best. Anne introduces Henry to her mother, who greets him respectfully. She invites them in. They step inside, and John greets them in the corridor with his arms outstretched. The door closes.

\* \* \*

The villa is brand new, made of glass and steel. On the first floor, two lengths of creamy linen glide apart before an imposing French window.

Anne gazes at the view, stroking her round belly.

112

The coast outside is wild and deserted as far as the eye can see, bathed in magnificent sunlight. Behind her, leaning against the doorjamb, Henry releases the button controlling the curtains and watches Anne's face closely to gauge her reaction. In the centre of the enormous room, Anne's old suitcase sits on a large bed covered in grey satin. The furniture is fashionable, utterly new, the bedroom modern, functional, impeccable, seemingly straight from the pages of a design magazine. It lacks nothing – except, perhaps, a touch of human warmth.

Anne turns around and spreads her arms, inviting Henry to come to her. He is about to take his first step when he hesitates, questioningly. She moves slowly across the room to him, and he pulls her into his arms. He slowly slips down her body to the floor, feverishly kissing her body along the way. He hugs her swollen belly and hides his face in her dress. Anne strokes his hair and kneels in front of him. Henry lowers his eyes in shame. She lifts his chin until she catches his gaze. She smiles at him gently.

'Don't worry. We can, if you want to.'

He stares into her eyes, at once stern and fearful. Anne sighs affectionately, stands up and undoes the buttons of her dress, one by one. Henry, at her feet, watches her undress. He grimaces as if in pain. She slips the straps from her shoulders and her dress falls to the ground, revealing her swollen breasts. She slips both thumbs behind the elastic of her low-cut panties and lowers them, slowly, then sits on the bed and kicks her ankles free. Transfixed, Henry gazes at her sex, level with his eyes. Anne shifts back along the bed, lies on her back, bends her knees, digs her heels into the edge of the mattress and lets her thighs fall outwards, spread apart.

\* \* \*

It's raining. Anne, pregnant, is jogging on the sand along the shore, soaking wet and alone. In the villa, behind the monumental picture window overlooking the beach, Henry sits at a large table of dark wood. In deep concentration, he draws a child's face on a blank sheet of paper.

\* \* \*

It's night. The room's curtains are wide open. Anne is lying on the bed, bathed in the misty light of the moon. She is curled up, half-naked, asleep. Seated in a chair in a dark corner of the room, Henry watches her.

\* \* \*

The doorbell's shrill ringing cuts through the heavy torpor of the empty house. Anne appears at the top of the stairs. She dashes down two steps at a time and hurries to open the front door, overjoyed to have a visitor.

In the driveway, the delivery man has already started up his van. Crates of food have been left on the doormat. Out of breath and disappointed, Anne holds her belly as she watches the vehicle drive away. Sunk into the living-room couch, Henry watches her in silence. He hasn't moved.

\* \* \*

The sun shines fiercely. The long beach is deserted. Dressed in an orange bathing costume, Anne plays in the breakers, laughing freely. Her belly is prominent. On the edge of the shore, Henry, fully dressed, skips to avoid the little waves that chase his leather shoes.

\* \* \*

A protective sheet is suspended from the glass ceiling. Dozens of stacked paintings lean against the plaster walls. The drawing table is strewn with half-finished sketches of children, crayons, opened tubes of coloured paint, dirty paintbrushes, stained rags. In front of the shuttered window, Henry touches up a painting placed on an easel. Completely absorbed, he meticulously checks the shadow cast by a dimple in a little girl's cheek. The child's face is taking shape; it seems almost alive. Anne enters the room and walks over to Henry, who continues working. She leans over him, kisses him on the neck and studies the canvas.

'You've made amazing progress.'

Henry smiles proudly as Anne thoughtfully examines the portrait.

'Where would you be without me?'

Henry raises his eyebrows and shrugs, laughing quietly without saying a word. Anne puts her head on his shoulder and sighs.

\* \* \*

Everything is white, sterile. Anne is crying in a hospital bed, large dark circles around her eyes. Next to her breast is the wrinkled face of a newborn baby, deep in sleep. A thread of milk drips from its open mouth. Sitting on the bed, Henry beams with joy.

\* \* \*

The car speeds down a country lane. Henry is rambunctious at the wheel.

'The saleswoman told me it's the best there is. She can't choke on it, and she can wear it up to eighteen months.'

He chatters on, transformed. On the back seat the Moses basket is belted, and beside it, Anne, tormented. She watches the road slip by without paying attention to him. Henry straightens up and glances in the rear-view mirror.

'Anne? Are you listening to me?'

'What? Yes.'

Henry raises his eyebrows, surprised at her lack of interest. He continues.

'So what do you think? If you don't like it, it's not a problem. I've kept the receipt and we can take it back –'

Anne cuts him off.

'Henry.'

'Yes.'

'I'm not staying. I've already bought my ticket. I'm going home.'

Henry takes his foot off the pedal. The car slows.

'I told you from the start. I never said I was going to move in with you permanently. I need to get back to work and take care of my baby. My mother's offered to help me.'

Henry's face falls.

'What do you mean, you want to leave? I've got everything set up.'

117

Anne remains silent as tears well in the corners of her eyes. Henry grits his teeth.

'Can I come with you?'

Anne tries to swallow past the lump in her throat, gulps with difficulty.

'I'm sorry, Henry. I need to be alone for a while. We'll come and see you during the holidays. I promise. I'll write.'

* * *

Anne jolts, startled. She's back sitting on her corpse, her eyes bulging and her face covered in tears. In front of her, high flames lick the sky, hiding Tsepel as he continues his prayers.

'You will go wherever your *karma* calls you, to any place and time of your life, but you will settle nowhere. Then you will be angry but it will do you no good. Since you cannot control anything, such emotions are pointless . . .'

Anne sobs and responds aggressively to Tsepel, furious.

'What else could I have done? Should I have become a recluse, locked away in his fortress? I had to think of Lucy. I couldn't have taken it even on my own. I had to get out and live my life.'

My God, I'm talking to myself. I'm going mad.

Anne sniffs and wipes away her tears.

'. . . If you are suffering, you must not blame any-one. It is your own *karma*.'

\* \* \*

The window is closed. The lilac outside has shed its leaves. A cold sunlight filters into the room. Anne is sitting on the bedspread printed with kites, next to an old cradle pushed into the shade. Silently she watches the sleeping Lucy suck her little thumb.

\* \* \*

An abandoned factory, converted into artists' stu-dios. Amid the curtains and screens, painters, sculptors and visual artists are at work, surrounded by posters, odd objects in strange compositions, complex assemblages. The factory is manufactur-ing again, art now its output.

Guided by a bearded man in his forties, Anne walks down the intricate assembly line. Lucy is strapped to her belly, sitting in a multicoloured shawl slung like a hammock. Wide awake, her head held up, she looks around with a ceaseless curios-ity. Her hair has grown, covering her skull with a silky down.

They climb a spiral staircase and disappear through the ceiling. On the next floor, a door is open at the end of a long corridor. The man invites Anne to go in. Flooded with light from a skylight, the room is about twenty square metres. It's empty. Exalted, Anne turns to her host, takes his hand, lifts it to her lips and kisses it in thanks.

\* \* \*

Photos of Lucy, a drawing of Henry and a mono-chromatic painting are fixed to the studio walls. Underneath, stacked wine crates have been recycled as bookshelves, kitchen cabinets, a storage space. A little refrigerator hums in a corner. On top of it next to the plug sit an electric kettle and a small stereo playing Bach's *St Matthew Passion*. A baby's play-pen has pride of place in the middle of the room on the large Berber rug. Lucy is comfortably installed on her backside behind the pale wooden bars, babbling away while fingering a cardboard book. Anne's work table, a long wood-fibre door resting on trestles, stands in front of the window. Whitish smoke rises from a black, cast-iron pot. Anne draws in wax the contours of an Egyptian cobra goddess on a canvas stretched tight and tacked to a rect-angular wooden frame. A young woman with a shaved head peers round the door and calls to her. Anne turns, smiling.

\* \* \*

Blue snowflakes drift into the glow of the street lights and settle neatly on the cotton-wool ground. A steaming car waits at the end of the driveway. Rose is standing at the front door, Lucy in her arms, wrapped up in her sleepsack. Anne skips out of the door, stopping to gently kiss Lucy on her head.

* * *

Anne's decorations, the photos of Lucy and the drawing of Henry, have now been overwhelmed by dozens of batik prints of every size and colour. They hang like patchwork from floor to ceiling, covering every centimetre of wall, darkening the room with menacing divinities. Mysterious animals sit beside trees of life, terrible faces, wrathful demons, inscrutable angels. Between the representation of Ganesh[9] as a child and the open mouth of a Melanesian crocodile hangs a portrait of Henry, the only human figure. His features are rigid and strained. His expression is enigmatic and ambiguous, at once warm and chilly, distracted and penetrating. Like the deities that surround him, he

---

[9] Hindu god of wisdom, intelligence and knowledge, Ganesh is portrayed with a human body and the head of an elephant.

seems to belong to a world of fantasy, outside time, beyond reach.

Anne sits at the work table, addressing empty envelopes. Into each she slips a card with a small reproduction of one of her batiks, a white wolf baring its fangs. On the back is written, in capital letters: 'RESURGENCE'. Beneath it: her name, a place, two dates, a time. These are the invitations to her first exhibition.

* * *

The gallery is packed, crowded with eccentric artists and bourgeoisie alike, excited children running about. The atmosphere is warm, punctuated with the clink of champagne glasses. Every now and again laughter rises above the hubbub. The batik prints are hung from the walls, their colours bursting under the lights. At the front is Henry's portrait. It's as if he were a king in attendance at his court of monstrosities.

In a corner of the room, Anne is chattering enthusiastically. Her black evening dress is fitted at the hips. Its bold, low neckline highlights the pearly curves of her nursing breasts. Her dishevelled chignon seems now to enhance her bearing. She is radiant, transformed, impressive, as if her new appearance is her unveiled true self.

Near the entrance, protected between her grandparents' legs, Lucy crawls around the floor. She
leaves her handprints on the misted window.

* * *

Daylight struggles through the haze of an overcast
sky. In the traffic-jammed avenue, the car's head-
lights are on full. Anne runs along the pavement and
rushes into the gallery. The walls of the room are
bare. Only Henry's portrait remains. On the counter
is an enormous bouquet of white camellias, next to a
magnum of champagne and two fluted glasses.

'Frank? Are you here?'

A neat young man sways out of an adjacent
room. Anne goes up to him impatiently.

'What the hell happened?'

He saunters to the counter, taking the bottle and
twisting off the wire cap.

'Like I told you on the phone, a collector came in
and bought them all. Except for that one.'

He sniffs at the solitary unsold work. The cork
pops, followed by a spray of foam.

* * *

The stereo is playing the allegro from a Bach violin concerto. The air rings slightly with a faint

tinnitus whistle. Anne is in her workshop tidying up her pigments; behind her, in the playpen, Lucy bangs a wooden drumstick against a coloured xylophone. From the doorway Henry watches her in silent admiration. He's wearing his customary suit, but set off by a new, improbably bushy beard. He knocks on the doorframe. Anne turns around. She looks at him for an instant, lost, then smiles broadly and opens her arms to welcome him.

'My God, look at you! When did you get here?'

Henry moves towards her.

'Last night.'

Anne hugs him affectionately.

'Why didn't you come to the opening?'

Henry kisses her on the cheek and gently extricates himself from her embrace.

'I came by, but there were too many people.'

Anne shakes her head disapprovingly.

'You haven't changed. Always the old recluse.'

Henry smiles placidly and turns his gaze towards Lucy, who has been watching them without moving.

'Say, how would you like to come and rest for a week by the sea? It's so beautiful in the spring.'

Anne frowns. Henry crouches in front of the playpen and offers his hand to Lucy through the bars.

'You can bring your boyfriend if you like.'

Anne is startled.

'How do you know I have a boyfriend?'

Too busy making faces at Lucy, Henry hasn't noticed the changed tone and answers evenly.

'I waited for you in front of your parents' place this morning. I didn't want to ring the bell. I was frightened I'd wake Lucy. So I waited and then the two of you came out. So I figured –'

Anne cuts him off angrily.

'So now you're stalking me?'

Surprised, Henry stands up and looks her in the eye.

'No, of course I'm not stalking you. What's up with you? Why are you so touchy? I'm just inviting you to spend a few days by the sea with your daughter and your boyfriend, that's all. You have time now, don't you?'

'What about my show?'

Henry turns his face to Lucy and nods unconvincingly.

'True.'

Anne stares at him, then, hesitantly, shakes her head slowly, with a rueful smile on her lips.

'I don't believe it . . .'

Anne takes a few steps back and bumps into her desk. Her voice quavers.

'You're the one who bought all my prints, aren't you?'

Trying to keep calm, Henry shuts his eyes, sighs, opens them and nods.

'Yes. I wanted them all.'

Anne cannot hold back her tears. She sobs.

'I should have guessed.'

Henry watches her anxiously.

'Why are you so upset?'

Anne pulls herself together. She snuffles and wipes her nose with the back of her hand.

'Why did you do it? What right do you have to interfere? Everything's over between us, do you hear me? It's over!'

Henry listens to her, frozen.

'. . . I felt sorry for you and tried to help, and you took advantage of it. I should never have accepted your invitation to Cape Cod. It was a trap! I thought I could help you, and I tried. With all my strength, for four long months, I tried. But it didn't do any good, none. Your misery and your – your inertia were stronger than me. You were suffocating me. I couldn't breathe around you!'

Henry steps back, trembling, unable to respond.

'Do you understand what I'm saying?'

Choking with sobs, Anne points to the door. Henry keeps retreating.

'Get out of here! Get out of my life and leave me alone!'

Henry's heel bumps into the wine crates. His

hands grope feverishly behind his back, his fingers brushing against some trinkets until they close around a small sculpture. Suddenly, his arm shoots up and out. The chiselled stone flies across the room and strikes Anne on her forehead. She collapses, blood spilling across the floor. Lucy is crying. Henry gathers her up and runs stiffly away.

\* \* \*

The saloon sweeps out of the steep cul-de-sac against sheets of rain. A rubbish truck pulls up in the alley, blocking the way. Henry slams on the breaks. The tyres lock and the car skids. Slowly, as though weightless, Lucy slips between the loose straps of the seat belt. She flies off the back seat and bumps limply against the felted roof. In front of her, the sheet metal hood of the car crumples under the steel mass. To her left, Henry's face plunges into the activated airbag. Head first, Lucy flies over the headrest, the passenger seat, the glove compartment, and smashes against the windscreen.

\* \* \*

Soaked, Anne hammers on the window of the resuscitation room. Henry limps into the corridor and halts at the sight of her. Aside from his arm in a sling and the plaster over his eyebrow, he is unscathed. Anne freezes and stares at him for a few seconds. He comes closer. She turns and squeezes her fists to control her rage. Henry comes up to her.

'How is she?'

Anne turns to him slowly, her mouth white. Henry shakes his head imploringly.

'I'm sorry, I didn't want this.'

Anne's hand strikes his face. She screams.

'Shut up!'

Henry hesitates. Anne slaps him again.

'Fuck off!'

Henry slumps against the wall. A male nurse runs over.

'Calm down, please! There are sick people trying to sleep.'

It's Evan, or rather, it's Evan as he was. He is barely recognisable, his expression detached, concerned, impersonal.

Henry straightens up and rubs his cheek. He has the hurt eyes of a child unfairly punished. His lips quiver in an inverted half-moon and he starts to cry.

Anne stares at him with contempt, whispering venomously, 'I despise you! Get away from me!'

'Come on, sir. I don't think this is the right time.'

Evan takes Henry by the elbow. Henry jerks out of his grasp, turns around and leaves.

\* \* \*

Anne sits up like a jack-in-the box. On her corpse she is panic-stricken, dripping with sweat, bombarded by the heat of the midday sun. Tsepel is there across from her, tirelessly stoking the fire. He is still reciting.

'You will want to enter your old body but it will already be rotten, useless . . .'

Evan is lying in the shade of tree. Apathetically, he listens to Bach, or what's left of it. The sound weeps from the headphones. The batteries are almost flat.

'. . . You are dead and it is too late to go back. Distance yourself from your former body, renounce it and be free.'

Anne gets up abruptly and shouts, 'Leave me alone! I don't give a fuck about being free!'

She rushes over to the fire and tries to kick the old man in anger, but her leg passes through him and she falls over backwards, her head landing in the fire.

\* \* \*

After Henry disappears round the end of the

corridor Anne slowly slides down the wall, sobbing. She collapses on the floor. Evan rushes to her and pulls her upright, putting an arm around her shoulder to soothe her.

'Easy now. Your daughter's going to make it.'

He rocks her gently, stroking her back.

'Calm down. It's over. Calm down.'

Anne hiccups in pain.

'Come on, let's have a look at this forehead.'

* * *

Shadows shift across the ceiling.

'Your daughter has suffered a severe cranial trauma . . .'

The doctor's voice is calm and reassuring.

Anne is sitting listlessly with her back to the window, brooding over the doctor's diagnosis, moving gently back and forth in her rocking chair. Her dressing gown is open, its tails hanging beneath the armrests, smacking against the legs of the chair.

'. . . She has what we call a subdural haematoma, a sort of blood clot in the brain. It should get reabsorbed, but in the meantime it would be best to keep a close eye on her. No more shocks, especially not to the head . . .'

Her eyes sunk into their sockets, the bags beneath them waxy, Anne stares listlessly at the cot. Her long hair is scraped back into a ponytail, accentuating the hard lines of her face.

'. . . Given the position of the lesion, it's possible that it will slow her psychomotor development a little, but don't worry. In her present condition, there's no reason to think there will be any long-term effects . . .'

Lucy sleeps peacefully in her cot, a thick band of gauze wrapped around the top of her head.

\* \* \*

Lucy, her head bandaged, is sitting in her high chair in the kitchen. Facing her in her nightdress, Anne delicately wipes her daughter's lips, removing the escaped residue of orange purée. Hiccuping, Lucy is sick. In horror Anne leaps up from her stool and lets out a panicked moan. Rose dashes into the kitchen, vainly trying to calm her daughter's hysteria. Anne hurtles blindly round the table, terrified at her powerlessness.

\* \* \*

Thirty-six point eight. Frowning, Anne stares worriedly at the old thermometer for an instant before shaking it back down to room temperature. Lucy is lying in front of her on the changing table. Wedged

131

between her mother's belly, two tiled walls and the back of a cupboard, she is surrounded. No way for her to fall.

The telephone rings. Anne takes a step back and stretches out an arm to take the receiver without moving away from her daughter.

'Hello. It's Henry.'

Anne doesn't move, doesn't respond, is expressionless. She refuses to speak.

'Anne, please answer me.'

* * *

Bent over the examination table, the doctor glides his icy stethoscope over the baby's abdomen. Lying on her back, Lucy giggles, free now from her bandaged turban. The doctor turns to Anne with a grin.

'Well! Your little girl is doing wonderfully. There's nothing to –'

'Careful!'

Anne rushes to the table to secure Lucy. Surprised by her anxiety, the doctor looks at her in concern.

'Right. As I was saying, there's nothing to worry about.'

He watches Anne carefully. Her smile looks weary, her features worn. Her mobile telephone rings. She fidgets it out of her pocket and looks at the lit screen. Henry's name blinks on the blue background. She sighs and refuses the call with a jerk of her thumb. The doctor lightly inclines his head, concerned.

'And what about you. How are *you* doing?'

* * *

Sitting at a thick mahogany table, an elegant man jots down notes with a gold-nibbed fountain pen. A crimson-and-gold-striped tie blazes against his white shirt. Behind him there's a credenza desk of dark wood, on which sit law books and an old brass scale, and above that a framed law diploma. The man lifts his head.

'Are you married?'

On the other side of the table, Anne is seated in a Le Corbusier armchair. Her spine bent, her shoulders hunched, she twists her fingers in search of courage.

'No.'

'Has he recognised the child?'

'No. It's not his.'

She replies flatly, without delay. This has to go quickly, no retreat or hesitation. This is the last obstacle. She has to surmount it.

The lawyer looks at her, surprised and satisfied.

'Well then, the matter is settled.'

* * *

A protective wreath of brilliant green sponge lines the bathtub. Sitting in a few centimetres of water, Lucy is gnawing on a rubber giraffe. Rose is kneeling in front of her, soaping her back. She speaks quietly.

'You shouldn't do this to him. It's not right.'

Standing behind her Anne blanches. Without saying a word, she turns on her heels and leaves the bathroom, slamming the door.

\* \* \*

Anne and her lawyer sit opposite an unoccupied defence bench. The courtroom is empty. The judge is on the dais, flanked by a clerk and a bailiff. He's wearing a black robe lined with white fur, a stiff collar and bands, also white, and an old rolled wig. He is getting ready to announce his verdict.

'The accused is not present?'

Anne's lawyer stands.

'No, your honour. He hasn't replied to any of our summonses and has refused the services of a court-appointed lawyer.'

The judge sighs.

'All right. Taking into account the circumstances that have been revealed, the court finds in favour of the plaintiff . . .'

Anne lowers her eyes.

'. . . By virtue of the powers vested in me, from this day forward the accused is forbidden from approaching or attempting to contact the plaintiff and her daughter, by any means whatsoever . . .'

Her head sinks.

'. . . Furthermore, and at the risk of future penalties, the accused must pay the plaintiff the sum of fifty thousand dollars in damages for the physical and moral harm done to her daughter. I declare this case closed.'

The judge's gavel strikes the block.

\* \* \*

The air throbs slightly, buzzing against her skin. Hanging on the wall is one of the batiks from Anne's show: an Egyptian god with a man's body and the head of a ram, large horns curling down to his shoulders. Anne sits beneath it on the floor, hunched up with her arms crossed over her head. Her hair is short. She's wearing the white shirt, the one she was wearing in the accident. Slowly she lowers her arms and opens her eyes.

What? Why am I here?

Above her, a large white sheet shades the room. Paintings are stacked floor to ceiling, ready to be sorted. Anne straightens up. The studio is a tip. Everywhere, strewn on the floor and on the

135

furniture, are dirty clothes, the remains of meals, broken glass, discarded balls of paper, broken frames, signs of struggle and neglect.

Henry is sitting at the far end of the studio, drawing. His beard has grown longer, as has his dishevelled hair.

Silent tears begin to roll down Anne's cheeks. The telephone rings, and after a few trills Henry picks it up.

'Hello?'

'Hello. It's Rose.'

Her voice is tremulous. Anne gets up and slowly walks towards Henry, wiping away her tears. His face is still. Anne can read his thoughts, feel his emotions. He knows something is wrong. He's worried, but he stays calm.

'Hi, Rose. Is something the matter?'

Rose snuffles at the other end of the line.

'Anne's had an accident.'

Henry sits forward and the hairs on his arms stand up. He'd guessed something but now it's going to be confirmed. Anne is dead; but he must think of Rose and John. He mustn't show his pain. He swallows, clears his throat and steadies himself.

'She's dead?'

Rose sobs on the other end of the line.

'Yes.'

Henry pauses. He has to stay calm, even at the risk of seeming indifferent. It's so hard. He breathes in through his nose and tries to set his pain aside in order to listen. That's his job. That's why Rose has called him. She needs to talk and he's the one she's chosen. He has to hold on, he can't crack.

'She had a motorbike accident. We've only just heard . . . They came off the road in the middle of the mountains . . . They fell into a precipice. Anne was killed. Evan broke his leg . . . The rescue crew took ten days to find them.'

Henry remains impassive. What can he say? How can he respond?

Lucy! Yes, Lucy is the answer. Lucy is life. Life goes on. You have to talk about life.

'Have you told Lucy?'

'No.'

The answer is frank, non-evasive. Rose cannot, does not want to do it. Lucy will be too young to understand, but Rose refuses to inflict on her the sight of her grandmother falling apart. Rose needs help. She needs his strength. Why does she trust him? Henry is losing himself in questions.

Does she really need me? Or is it my ego getting carried away?

He has no idea what path to follow, but Rose is waiting. He must say something.

Anne kneels down and urges him on.

'Go on, Henry, go on. Think! You can figure this out.'

Henry closes his eyes and starts to breathe again.

*Who am I to say no to her? How could I refuse if I can help her?*

Anne smiles as Henry reopens his eyes.

'Would you like me to come over?'

'I'd really appreciate it. John's losing it and I'm struggling on my own . . . Could you come for a few days, take care of Lucy?'

Henry gasps for air. Rose has asked him. She's asked him. He has to hold on for a few seconds more.

'I'll set off immediately. I'll be there tonight.'

'Thank you.'

The line goes dead. Henry hangs up and remains motionless.

'Henry?'

The buzzing has stopped.

'You're free, Henry. Go ahead.'

Henry picks up his charcoal again. Anne tries to take his hand. It glides through him, but he stops still. Anne draws her hand back. Henry puts down his charcoal and lifts his head, looking at the picture frame on the table in front of him. The photograph is of Anne in her studio. She's standing barefoot on the floorboards, her hair unkempt. Her dress is deep red, half-length, with a wide collar and a pattern of lotus flowers across the front. She is smiling radiantly. In her arms, against her breast, Lucy is wrapped in a beige alpaca poncho. At the top left corner of the photograph, a few words are scribbled in black marker: 'My new studio. See you soon. Love from us both.'

Anne rises, leans her face towards Henry's and places a kiss on his cheek.

'Thank you, Henry. Please forgive me for all the pain I caused you.'

Henry smiles as he looks at the photograph.

\* \* \*

Dusk covers the valley. The parasol pine is coloured pink by the setting sun. Evan's head rests against the trunk. He tries with painful swallows to eat a mouthful of food. His eyes are stinging. His eyelids blink wearily, too heavy to stay open.

'You know . . . she is . . . my life.'

He's babbling. His sentences are dislocated, their rhythm dictated by his halting breath. He is delirious with exhaustion.

In front of him, Tsepel nods sympathetically as he carefully scrapes the bottom of a sachet of freeze-dried mash.

'It's almost empty.'

Anne sits beside him, trying to hold onto the relief from her vision of Henry to soften the jolts of pain she feels within Evan.

Tsepel holds out the spoon.

'Last one.'

Evan giggles hoarsely.

'Do you . . . believe in . . . destiny?'

Tsepel nods soothingly.

'I don't.'

Seeing an opportunity, Tsepel takes advantage of Evan's half-open mouth and slips the spoon between his lips. Evan continues his weak chuckling as he slowly chews the mush that sticks against the walls of his dry mouth. Silent tears run down his cheeks. Anne sighs.

'Why are you hurting yourself like this? It's not your fault.'

Anne gets up, goes to Evan, sits in his lap and hugs him.

'You've got to stop wallowing. Remember the times we had. You made me happy.'

She closes her eyes and concentrates.

\* \* \*

It's pouring with rain in Central Park. Anne is soaked. She runs behind the pushchair, its hood up. Lucy is tucked under her mother's raincoat, the ladybird helmet securely fastened round her head. A man passes them in the other direction, protected by an umbrella. He stops, turns around and runs back to catch up with them.

'Excuse me!'

Anne turns. The umbrella lifts and she recognises Evan's lean face. His serious expression is offset by his cheerful voice.

'Do you remember me? From the hospital . . . your daughter's accident?'

\* \* \*

The sheer curtains at the open bay window waft slowly in the gentle summer breeze. Outside on the street below a group of young boys admires a large motorbike. Anne leans against the doorframe, watching Evan sit with Lucy as she beats a small drum on the carpet in the living room. Lucy strikes Evan's hand with the drumstick.

'Owww!'

Evan makes a face of exaggerated pain and shakes his hand dramatically, as Lucy squeals with delighted laughter. Evan looks at her, pleased, and raises his eyes to Anne. She smiles at him.

'Do you like music?'

\* \* \*

Large storm clouds drift across the sky. Bunches of campanula blooms sprawl in the shady undergrowth. The rich soil is damp. Evan is strolling with Anne and Lucy, who is buckled into her pushchair and still wearing her ladybird helmet. They are wearing summer clothes. Anne is talking passionately.

'. . . He said that Bach is the only thing that suggests the universe isn't a failure, and also the only plausible proof of God's existence. And yet he was a convinced atheist. Pretty funny, don't you think?'

Evan agrees with a smile. Anne stops suddenly.

'Am I boring you?'

Evan looks up at the sky and points at a treetop.

'Look!'

Anne lifts her head. While she is looking Evan pushes her and, caught off balance, she slips and falls into a puddle.

'Are you crazy?'

Evan bursts out laughing; so does Lucy.

'Bastard!'

\* \* \*

John is holding a ladybirded Lucy in his arms as Anne bends over to kiss her. Her hair is cut short. She's taken care with her appearance.

'Please don't let her out of your sight, okay?'

John nods confidently. Anne scrunches her nose up at Lucy and then runs out across the garden. On the other side of the hedge, Evan is waiting for her on his motorbike.

\* \* \*

The soprano begins the Last Supper aria from Bach's *St Matthew Passion*. Anne and Evan are sitting in the middle of the church among an otherwise silver-haired audience. Anne cranes her neck to see the singer better. She has tears in her eyes. At her side, Evan watches her with an affectionate smile.

\* \* \*

The loft's plain windows are ineptly plastered into rusting steel frames. A garden table, four cafe chairs, a rush mat and a coat rack are the room's only furniture. Amid a scattering of discarded clothes, Anne and Evan have fallen asleep curled up together on the floor, photos of batiks strewn around them. At the far end of the room, tucked up on a mattress between two cushions, Lucy is also fast asleep.

\* \* \*

143

Dressed in white scrubs, Evan walks down a long hospital corridor. Anne darts out of a recess and catches him by the sleeve, dragging him to the wall and pressing herself against him. From her pushchair Lucy watches them curiously.

* * *

A shirt partially covers a pizza that has been scarcely touched. Other clothes are scattered across the floorboards. On the bed, Anne and Evan are naked, entwined.

* * *

The Pen Station platform is crowded as the departure whistle sounds. Hanging out of the entrance to the compartment, Evan kisses Anne. The door closes and the train starts to pull away. Anne waves, tears rolling down her cheeks.

* * *

A saucepan of molten wax, cantings[10] and a wooden frame are placed on the kitchen table. Anne stands

---

[10] Tools for applying the hot wax to the fabric.

in front of the cauldron busily boiling away on the hob. Armed with a long wooden stick and protected behind a sleeved apron, she extracts a thick, crumpled length of fabric, which drips dark red.

* * *

Upstairs in her room, Anne lifts Lucy by her legs and places a nappy under her bottom. Downstairs, the telephone rings. Rose picks it up.

'Anne, it's for you!'

'Coming!'

Anne pats Lucy's tummy.

'Don't you move. I'll be right back.'

Anne hurries out of the room, dashes down the stairs and takes the phone.

'Hello?'

'Good day, madam, sorry to bother you. My name is Ajeet and I'm a friend of Evan's.'

The man speaks with a strong accent.

'I have been trying to reach him for several days without success. At the hospital they said you might be able to help me.'

Taken aback, Anne frowns, glances upstairs and answers quickly.

'I wish I could help you but I don't really know where he is either. He said he was going travelling for a few weeks. He'll be back soon.'

'You don't know the name of the place?'

'I'm afraid not. I'm sorry, I've got to go. My baby's waiting for me. Bye.'

'Thank you. Goodbye.'

Anne hangs up and hurries back to the bedroom.

\* \* \*

The Christmas tree is resplendent. In the middle of the living room, Anne sits cross-legged on the carpet, daintily untying the yellow ribbon round a present's crimson silk wrapping paper. Behind her, in the kitchen, Lucy babbles joyfully, encouraged by her grandmother. Anne pulls back the wrapping paper to uncover a beautiful book, *Tangkas: Buddhist Paintings from Tibet*. Anne opens it and leafs through it slowly. A thick envelope slips out of the pages and falls in her lap. Anne picks it up, opens it and pulls out two plane tickets: New York–Kolkata. Leaning against the marble mantelpiece, Evan watches her adoringly. His hair has grown; he has fleshed out, got a tan. He looks like a new person.

\* \* \*

Muffled voices spill out of the loudspeakers and blend with the deafening noise of the crowd on a busy day at JFK International Airport. In front of the customs desk, Anne hugs Lucy one last time before entrusting her into her father's arms. The officer hands back their passports. Evan takes them and taps his watch, looking at Anne: it's time to go. Anne gives a last round of kisses to her parents and her daughter, then turns around and walks into the departure lounge.

\* \* \*

The morning mist hovering over the ground is set alight by the rising sun. Anne is stretched out on her corpse, her eyes wide open, gazing at the clear orange sky above her.

It's so beautiful . . . What if I stayed here, completely still? What could happen to me?

The snapping of a twig fractures the silence and Anne turns her head towards the sound. A few metres away Tsepel approaches, his arms laden with dead branches. He drops his bundle onto the existing pile and sits down heavily, taking a rag from his pocket to wipe his forehead. The fire in front of him breathes its last.

What's he waiting for? Why doesn't he put more on?

Anne sighs. Evan is beside her, pressed up against her remains. The gauze bandages holding his splint are a filthy grey, some of them unravelling. Anne watches him calmly. His breathing is short and wheezy and his face is filthy, coarsened beneath layers of grime. His hair bunches into oily petals. His scraggly new beard makes him look like a castaway.

'My darling, you don't look very well. I'm really sorry, you know . . . I'm so sorry I got you into all this.'

Anne strokes his cheek with the back of her hand. Evan immediately scratches the spot.

'You can feel me? Am I tickling you? Is that it?'

Anne smiles and curls up against him. Evan's eyes suddenly start open. Drawing on his last reserves of strength, he props himself up on one elbow and, shading his eyes from the low sun, scans the horizon. Other than Tsepel near the fire there isn't a soul in sight. Evan lifts the sleeping bag and recoils, gagging at the smell of the decomposing body. Anne is disfigured. Evan holds his breath and leans over to kiss her forehead.

'Hello . . . gorgeous.'

He rolls heavily onto his back.

'I just dreamt . . . of your little Lucy . . . She was floating in the air like a balloon . . . laughing . . .'

* * *

Two plump little feet totter onto a rich green lawn dotted with lily-of-the-valley. John is a few steps away on his knees, arms spread wide to welcome the new walker.

'Well done! That's good! Keep going!'

Lucy advances, her ash-blonde hair whipping in the wind. She stretches her hands out in front of her, teetering dangerously.

'Come on! Almost there!'

Heel and arch are lifted away from the ground, but the toes are lazy and drag in the grass. Lucy topples forward. John rushes to catch her in his arms.

'That's good, sweetie. Well done. You're getting there.'

In congratulation, in consolation, in encouragement, John tosses her into the air and up she flies, like a helium balloon. She comes back down and is then shot up again, shrieking with joy. John catches her and rolls her in his arms.

'Shall we try again?'

Lucy regards him beatifically. John pops her down onto the lush green carpet and retreats a few steps, kneeling down to resume his welcoming position, and claps his hands together.

'Come on now! Here we go!'

Lucy begins her perilous journey again, takes a few steps and tumbles over. John leans forward

149

and tickles Lucy in the ribs, smiling as she wriggles and squeals. He stands up and, back bent, takes her by the hand, walking with her a few steps before letting go. Lucy walks on, all on her own, lifting her hips high. Two new arms snatch her up just before she falls.

'Brilliant!'

Laughing, Henry hugs Lucy. John looks on approvingly.

'Oh, good. You can take over now.'

Patting Henry on the shoulder, John heads towards the house, striding past a brand-new set of swings where Evan sits. His right leg, in a cast, rests on the handle of one of his crutches. Rose is beside him.

'You'll have supper with us before you go, won't you?'

Her voice is gentle, but she shoots Evan an insistent look. He laughs, amused.

'With pleasure. But I can't stay late. I'm on call tonight.'

'Lovely. And you, Henry?'

Henry looks quizzically at Lucy. She stares back, expressionless. Henry nods.

'Yes. I suppose that means yes.'

Rose smiles.

'Thank you.'

She gets up and goes to join John indoors. Henry

sits down on the lawn and gathers Lucy onto his lap. Anne is sitting on the grass nearby. She watches them, enthralled, as Lucy tugs at Henry's nose. A rumble of thunder sounds in the distance and the sky grows suddenly dark. Lucy rolls off Henry's knees and crawls away on the grass.

'I would have loved to hold you in my arms . . .'

Lucy stops and turns her head in Anne's direction, as if she has heard her.

'. . . I would have loved to do so many things with you . . .'

Lucy stares straight at the place where her mother is standing.

'. . . But you're going to have to walk without me, my love. And you will walk . . .'

The little girl watches Anne, her head wagging.

'. . . And you'll keep laughing too . . .'

Lucy's face breaks into an instantaneous toothy smile. The thunder rumbles again and Lucy looks up.

'. . . You'll laugh so hard that I'll hear you . . .'

A raindrop splashes onto Lucy's cheek.

\* \* \*

Anne is lying on her side, her eyes scrunched up.

'. . . Wherever you are, I'll hear you.'

Anne opens her eyes and looks around her. She is in the ravine, curled up against Evan. He has gone back to sleep.

'You'll go and see her from time to time, won't you? And you'll tell her about me?'

Evan's breathing chirrs and catches, wheezy with incipient bronchitis.

'Thank you.'

Anne lays a worried kiss on his cheek, sits up and turns towards the old man. He is lying beside the extinguished fire, also asleep. She gets up and walks over to kneel in front of him.

'Sir.'

Tsepel does not react. Anne moves her hand towards his shoulder to try to shake him awake.

'Sir, wake up!'

Her hand passes through him.

'Shit!'

Anne sinks her fist inside his body and twists it vigorously.

'Come on, wake up!'

A spasm shakes Tsepel's shoulder. He opens his eyes. In front of him, his legs covered by the tunic, Evan is lying next to the corpse, unmoving, as though dead. Reassured, the old man lies down and goes back to sleep.

You've got to be kidding me.

'Sir, please, you have to go and get help for Evan. He's sick –'

She's interrupted by a dog's bark. She turns around and far off she can just make out a dog running towards her through the brush. It is indistinct against the glowing light behind it. Anxiously Anne begins to back up, trying to shade her eyes from the glare of the early-morning sun. Walking backwards, she passes first through the remains of the dead fire and then through Evan, but she collides with her corpse and falls over backwards, landing on top of it. Hurriedly she struggles to get up, but after a moment she stops and her expression quickly changes.

'Hector?'

The dog is now just on the other side of the fire and there's no doubt: it's definitely a brown and white pointer.

'Hector!'

The dog jumps on her and enthusiastically licks her face. For a few moments Anne tries to pull him back by his collar but, bursting with joy, she kneels down and hugs him tightly.

'Hector, Hector, it's you!'

A shadow falls on them. Her grandfather stands above them, blocking the sun. He's wearing an impeccable black suit and a shirt so white, so dazzling that even in shadow it lights up his face.

153

'Hello, Anne.'

His voice is smooth and warm. Stupefied, Anne pushes a yapping Hector aside. She straightens up and sits on her corpse, staring at her grandfather in dumbfounded silence, tears flooding her eyes. He settles down beside her and grabs Hector, pushing him down to sit by his feet. Anne smiles warmly into his patient face. She hesitates a second and then hugs him with all her strength.

'You still smell the same . . . It's been so long.'

Anne relaxes her hold and looks back and forth between her grandfather and his dog.

'I'm so happy to see you again. You can't imagine how much I've missed you.'

Her grandfather smiles at her affectionately and nods his head in understanding.

'How are you?'

Anne turns her head away and gently pats Hector's muzzle.

'So-so.'

Her grandfather slips a finger under her chin and lifts it, as if she were a child. Anne lets him do it. She watches him thoughtfully for a few moments.

'I knew you weren't dead . . .'

He laughs.

'Really? And yet, when you were little, you had your doubts. You remember?'

Anne snuffles and smiles.

'Yes, of course I remember. I was dead too . . . I mean, not really dead . . . I don't know how to put it into words, but you must know anyway. It's like now. I'm dead, you're dead and so is Hector. Yet here we are, the three of us, as if we'd only just parted . . . And you recognised me straight away, even though you haven't seen me in twenty years.'

Her grandfather looks her straight in the eye.

'So how is it that I'm here now?'

Anne's smile turns to sadness, then fades entirely.

'I don't know . . . For now, I'm here and so are you. That's what matters, right?'

She lowers her eyes again.

'Please don't spoil this. You're going to make me cry.'

He puts out an arm, takes her hand and presses it between his palms.

'You see, I can touch you and you can touch me. You feel my hand, don't you? It's warm. You can pet Hector as well and even smell us. Yet we are all dead, and I'm not really here.'

Anne bites her lip to hold back the tears.

'Please stop.'

'I can't, Anne. You know I can't. You brought me here to tell you that. So you wouldn't be alone when you admit to yourself what you already know, so I could say it to you clearly and comfort you. I am your courage and your love. I am a part of you.'

Anne sniffs.

'You can't touch Evan, your parents, Lucy, Henry. Your paths have separated. You've left them.'

'Then why can I see them? Why can I hear them?'

'Would you have preferred it if everything ended suddenly, if they disappeared forever without you having the time to say goodbye?'

Anne smiles a little at herself and looks over at Evan. His ribcage swells stutteringly, then abruptly sags.

'It's true. I've seen them, I've spoken to them, I've told them that I love them . . . I've tried to comfort them . . . And I've asked for their forgiveness. I think they heard me. Yes, I believe they heard me.'

She turns to her grandfather.

'Don't you think?'

'Why do you keep asking me questions when you know the answers?'

Anne sighs.

'It's hard to accept.'

'Of course, but my being here means you've already accepted it . . . Are you ready to continue on your path?'

Anne frowns. Her grandfather raises her hand, kisses it sofly and blows the kiss towards her.

'You can't stay here forever. You finished what you had to do, right?'

Anne stares at him worriedly. He smiles back.

'Well, there's no need to look at me like that. You wanted to see us and you've seen us. You wanted to say goodbye to us and you've said goodbye. You're no longer afraid, so why not have faith?'

Evan begins to cough suddenly, startling Hector. Tsepel awakes and sits up, watching as Evan's head judders against the corpse's shoulder. Eventually the fit passes, without jogging Evan from his sleep. Tsepel rubs his face and takes up his prayer beads.

'Noble one, if you have not yet arrived at libera-tion, you will soon leave your old life and begin a new one . . .'

Anne smiles and turns to her grandfather.

'Are you two in cahoots or someth –'

He's disappeared. She twists her head, scanning the mountains for her grandfather and Hector. Not a trace: they've gone. Anne sighs.

'. . . You will see a man and a woman coupling. Whatever you do, do not come between them. You could become trapped in a uterus. Try instead to close the door of the womb. This will be your last chance to escape the suffering of a new existence.

There are five ways of closing the womb door. Remember them, because at any point they will enable you to refuse the path that your *karma* is pushing you towards, and to remain free to choose for yourself. First you should try to turn your thoughts away from the sexual act by thinking of the man and the woman as a spiritual master and his companion. Choose people you respect for their wisdom and goodness and ask them to share their teaching with you, and the womb should close on its own. If it does not, try to think of the mating couple as a representation of the primordial Buddha. This Buddha is deep within you. It is you, even if you do not know it. Concentrate and draw from it the spiritual strength to follow the path of awakening. If the womb still does not close, you will most likely fall under the sway of a powerful sexual attraction to one of the two in the couple, and a profound hatred and jealousy of the other. Chase away these negative feelings, for they will lead you into a new life of suffering. Gather all your strength to banish hatred and passion from your heart and mind. If this is too difficult, try to understand that what you see is merely a projection of your imagination, an illusion, and that this illusion will bring you only rootlessness and pain. If you can understand that these illusions are false and meaningless, the womb will close all by itself. If you cannot manage this, try the last method. Remember the pure light that you saw at the start of your journey through death. This light was the reflection of the nature of your spirit, completely empty, without beginning or end. Focus on that light and try to recover that emptiness, allowing your spirit to flow like pure water, relaxed and receptive. Should none of these techniques work, the womb door will close over you and you will be carried irretrievably towards the world of your rebirth. Do not panic. If you sense that the world you are being carried towards is unfavourable and one in which you do not wish to be reborn, concentrate on something positive. If you succeed, you are sure to be guided in the right direction. You cannot go wrong. Listen carefully to the directions that I give you now, for they will be the last and may spare you a rebirth into one of the inferior worlds.'

Evan is attacked by another coughing fit, stronger than the first. Tsepel stops speaking and looks in his direction. After several convulsions, Evan manages to swallow and quietens. Anne is sitting beside him. Powerless, she strokes his hair, hoping to soothe him.

'Please, I'm begging you, go and get help. He's exhausted. You have to take care of him.'

Preoccupied, Tsepel sighs.

'Hold on, young man, I've nearly finished with your wife. Afterwards, I'll take care of you.'

He resumes his swaying and chanting.

'. . . Noble one, listen to my last words of advice. During this final stage, you will have three choices to make. They will determine your sex, the place of your birth and the form of your next incarnation. The form that you take will depend on the world in which you are reborn. There are six worlds in all. Each corresponds to specific dwelling places. Feeling rushed, you will be tempted to seek refuge in the first reassuring shelter, but be careful. Do not hurry. This may be a trap on the part of your *karma*. Resist and seek the right path . . .'

Anne continues to stroke Evan's hair.

'Don't worry, my love. He knows you're not well. He's thinking of you, too.'

'. . . Each of these six worlds has its own distinctive colour. Pay attention to your body, because it will take on the colour of the world in which you will be reborn. If you arrive at a luxurious palace and your body turns white, you are entering the world of the gods. This is a world of illusions engendered by pride and self-centredness. If you enter a deep forest and see weapons or men fighting, and your body turns red, you are entering the world of the demigods. Beware of them. They are jealous, envious and spiteful. If you can, concentrate on closing the door to the womb and leave. If you find yourself in a crowd or in a city and your body turns blue, you will have the chance to be reborn among humans, a world dominated by self-ishness and desire. If your body turns green and you feel yourself wanting to enter caves, holes in the ground and nests, this means you are about to become an animal. If you can, avoid this world, for it is pitiless. Ignorance and the rule of strength prevail here. If you become yellow and feel the need to hide among tree stumps and deep caverns, you are approaching the world of the hungry spirits. Avoid this world, for those that live there suffer from greed and eternal dissatisfaction. Finally, if you are drawn towards hell, your being will turn grey as smoke and you will see black and red places, metallic constructions or wells. Avoid this world at all costs, for hatred and anger reign there, breeding unbearable tortures . . .'

Anne rises and approaches the old man.

'. . . Know that only one of these six worlds allows you to continue to progress. That is the world of humans. Its colour is blue. Remember this and pay attention, because the force of your *karma* may attract you towards another destiny . . .'

Anne kneels down in front of Tsepel.

'Sir, you have to take care of Evan now.'

'. . . Now I'm going to tell you how to choose the sex of your next incarnation . . .'

161

'Sir. Please. Thank you for your advice, but Evan is very sick. You must help him.'

'. . . As I have said, when you see your father and your mother in the process of conceiving you, you will feel jealousy towards one of them and a powerful carnal desire for the other. You will acquire the sex of the one you are jealous of . . .'

Anne is about to try to interrupt Tsepel again, but he leaves her no gap. She gives up and listens.

'. . . My last instructions concern the place of your birth. You could be reborn on any of the four continents.[11] If you are to be reborn in Asia, you will see many beautiful and welcoming houses. Do not hesitate to enter. This is the most favourable continent, the one that dispenses the teachings of the Buddha. The other three will present themselves to you in the form of lakes on whose shores animals have come to quench their thirst. If you see geese and ganders, you will be at the gates of Oceania. If you see stallions and mares, this will show you the way to Europe and Africa. And if you see a herd of cattle, you will be reborn in the Americas . . .'

Anne listens to Tsepel, entranced. She shakes her head, trying to break free from his hypnotic voice.

Evan, you have to take care of Evan.

'. . . You are now free to choose.'

---

[11] Buddhist texts refer to only four continents.

Anne claps her hand over Tsepel's mouth to silence him. He rubs his lips. Anne takes her hand away.

'I've heard you and I thank you. Now, please go and get help for Evan. He's the emergency. If you don't help him, he'll die.'

Tsepel raises his head. Evan is still asleep against Anne's corpse. He's not coughing any more but shivering, his breathing shallow and uneven. With sudden urgency Tsepel pockets his prayer beads, grabs his pouch and rummages inside it. He pulls out his water gourd, bits of dried meat, a folded handkerchief and a box of matches, methodically placing each item before him. He wraps the meat in the handkerchief and stands up, slipping the strap of his bag over his head. He bends down to gather the items from the ground and walks over to Evan. Kneeling in front of him, he places the gourd, the handkerchief and the matches near his face; then he takes the tunic, bundled messily at Evan's feet, shakes it out and covers Evan's chest with it. He takes out his prayer beads, lifts the sleeping bag and places them carefully between Anne's blue breasts.

'There is one last important thing. You may see people who are dear to you whom you have left behind. Do not become attached to them, because they could turn you away from your true path.

163

Concentrate on staying open and calm, without desire or repulsion, without passion or aggression.'

Evan painfully opens his eyes and smiles weakly at Tsepel beside him. The old man returns his smile, stands up and addresses him.

'I'm going to find a doctor to take care of you. He'll be here tomorrow. I've left you something to eat and to drink, and my matches too, so you can light the fire if you find the strength.'

Tsepel bows his head slightly, joins his hands at the level of his chin and respectfully takes his leave of Evan. He then simply turns on his heel and walks off quickly. For a moment Evan watches him go. Anne sits beside him.

'You'll see, he'll be back with help. Hang on. He won't be long.'

Evan's eyelids droop shut. Tsepel is battling up the slope of the ravine. He trips, grabs hold of some roots, starts off again, slips on some loose pebbles. White and black stones roll under his feet. They rush down the slope, dragging others along with them. In a few seconds, the few stones have become a rock slide. Black and white merge in a fluid and expanding grey mass that gathers and collects and becomes a heaving, roaring torrent.

Unmoving, Anne watches the wave rushing towards her. Neither thoughts nor fears disturb her. Serenely she is swept up and bobs at the surface like a cork, spinning in the passing eddies. Behind her, the ravine with Evan and her corpse fade quickly into the distance.

She speeds on through changing landscapes that blur into one another. Soon she has left the mountains and is rushing through plains, flying over cities, details smearing in a haze of speed. There's nothing left but water, sky and air, as far as the eye can see. A gigantic maelstrom takes shape on the horizon.[16] catches Anne in its spiralling arms. Her body begins to turn faster and faster, trapped in the whirlpool's revolutions, drawing her ever tighter into its centre. Without fear Anne lets herself be carried in, embracing the water with her arms outspread, relinquishing all control. Her spirit is free, ready to receive, open at last. The final spires sink into the black hole and Anne is swallowed up.

\* \* \*

Horns blare and down a road jammed with traffic. It's raining. Anne is lying on the pavement, drenched and unconscious. A hand shakes her shoulder.

'Madam?'

Anne opens her eyes. Next to her nose stands a perfectly polished pair of shoes on the wet concrete.

'Madam!'

Barely daring to move, Anne rolls slowly over. Leaning down is her father, holding an umbrella.

'Are you okay?'

Anne stares up at him, astounded.

'Dad? What are you doing here?'

John straightens up suddenly, taken aback.

'Do we know each other?'

Behind him, a woman tugs at the sleeve of his overcoat.

'Come on, can we go please?'

Anne raises herself on her elbow and sits up, smiling. She knows that voice.

'Rose, can you please just let go of me for a second?'

He turns, allowing Anne to glimpse past him at his wife.

'Can't you see she isn't well?'

Anne grins broadly. There's her mother, looking young and healthy, her face, like her husband's, showing no recognition of their daughter in front of her. Affably, John leans over Anne again and offers his arm.

'Here, take my hand.'

Terrified that her hand will pass right through his, Anne hesitates a moment before cautiously extending her fingers. They make contact with his warm skin and, overjoyed, she lifts her head and grasps his wrist firmly. He pulls her towards him and helps her up.

'Thank you.'

'You're welcome. Will you be all right now?'

Anne nods.

'Well, goodbye then.'

'Goodbye.'

John and Rose turn around and continue on, Rose's muttered grumble lost behind the noise of the traffic. Anne watches them walk away.

'Take care of yourselves!'

They disappear around the next corner. Anne wipes away the drops that fall on her face and looks around her. The road is lined on either side by red-brick buildings, and slowly Anne realises she recognises the street outside her studio. Over on the other side of the road, rubbish bins huddle in the corner of a dark and narrow cul-de-sac: the dead end where Lucy's accident happened. Anne stays calm, to her surprise. She has an odd feeling, both touched and emotionally detached, as if these memories belonged to another life, a life in which she tried her best, where she made mistakes, and got some things right. Now she's here again, with no idea what will happen. She is overwhelmed with intense joy, the joy of living in this moment, with neither regret for the past nor fear of the future. She has faith in those she's leaving behind.

She knows they will pull through without her, despite the pain and sorrow. Finally, she's at peace. She feels free like never before.

Everything seems normal, nothing out of the ordinary. Pedestrians walk by huddled under their umbrellas, talking, shopping. Young teenagers run around laughing. In the middle of the intersection, a policeman tries futilely to placate the car horns.

Anne marvels at this incredible mechanism, these bodies, these machines, the wind and the rain. She laughs, for she can hear the thoughts of the passers-by: they're wondering if she's crazy, standing there soaking wet and stock still in the rain. Anne doesn't worry. She's simply happy to be there, among them all.

A taxi pulls up in front of her and a young woman backs out of the passenger door, a little dishevelled. She's wearing scarlet boots, rainbow tights and a vibrant polyester raincoat. Anne shakes her head, intrigued. That hairstyle, those clothes . . . The woman turns around and Anne comes face to face with herself.

'Are you coming, Lucy?'

Lucy slips down from the back seat to the pavement all by herself. She's a few months older, maybe even a year older. Anne watches her daughter, bursting with pride. Lucy's golden hair is long and curly. She's no longer a baby, but a beautiful little girl. She looks up and smiles at Anne.

Do you recognise me?

Anne wonders but expects no answer. Even if Lucy did, what difference would it make? She is there and that is enough.

Hurriedly her double takes Lucy by the hand and crosses the road, zigzagging between the stationary cars. Over her shoulder Lucy continues to smile at Anne, inviting her to follow them. They walk into an apartment building, the heavy wrought-iron door thudding shut behind them. Anne thinks back to Tsepel's words: the trap of the reassuring shelter, do not enter the womb. But does she really want to avoid rebirth? Her mind is clear. She knows what she is risking, but she wants to keep going. This is where she must go. Calmly, of her own free will, she crosses the road. Her steps are deliberate, each one taking her further down the path she has chosen. She lifts her hand to the metal door and pushes it open to reveal an art nouveau lobby. Anne slips inside. Her double and Lucy are standing at the back, waiting in front of the gated lift. There's a loud bang as the outside door closes behind her. Lucy looks over her shoulder and her smile grows even wider as she sees Anne approach. The wooden cabin lift descends past the moulded high ceiling and stops level with the checkerboard floor tiles. The accordion door grille rattles open. Lucy and Anne's double enter the tight space and turn around to face Anne. Her double is waiting for her to make up her mind.

'Are you coming with us?'

Anne looks at her double, amused. She's talking to herself. She knows it.

'I'd love to.'

Anne winks conspiratorially at her daughter and enters the lift. The grille closes behind her and the cabin begins to rise up the shaft and into the building.

* * *

The lift door creaks open. Lucy steps out, followed by Anne. The double has disappeared.

They are in a long and narrow corridor on the top floor. Lucy walks on with a confident step. She seems to know her way around. Anne follows her, silently. When she has reached the end of the corridor, Lucy goes over to a window, where raindrops trickle slowly down the pane. Anne joins her at her side and together they look out of the window. Through the window on the opposite side of the courtyard they can see a couple embracing. She is naked, he clothed. Anne observes them, rapt, filling with envy as she watches the beautiful woman.

She's the one leading the dance. The door to the lift creaks again. Anne turns around. Lucy is standing by the lift, ready to leave. Anne raises her arm and waves. Lucy steps forward and the door closes behind her.

\* \* \*

Fingers slide stealthily beneath a shirt. The fabric slides off his shoulders. She undresses him.

Anne is with them, flattened against the wall, hypnotised.

The woman pushes the man onto the bed and straddles him. The bodies intertwine and turn over. He is above, she beneath him.

Anne is unmoving, like a statue. Her body turns blue and she smiles in expectation of her new life.

He enters her. She receives him. His back undulates, his skin tautens, his muscles clench and stiffen. They convulse and grimace.

Ecstasy. Anne radiates indigo. Her body, her eyes melt into the blue.

\* \* \*

The azure liquid is striped by rays of white light. The sun passes through limpid water. The surface

171

approaches. A lake appears. Horses quench their thirst on its shore.

* * *

There is no noise, not a sound. A halo glows in the darkness. Little by little, a lattice of tiny milky veins pulls away from the translucent membrane.

The light grows stronger to reveal the damp walls of a red-mottled cavity of flesh.

In the hollow of the fleshy chalice a drop of blood forms. Its shape is perfect, its surface lustrous and flawless. It seems to wait, immutable.

At the summit, a whitish fluid pierces the diaphanous tissue. A teardrop forms, hanging from the membrane. It expands until, too heavy, it breaks free and falls in a precise vertical. It crosses the purplish pocket without changing course, crashing straight into the drop of blood.

The two drops explode into a multitude of little beads, propelled out against the walls. They roll down towards the base, and reunite and merge, like mercury.

The cavity suddenly contracts and a dull sound reverberates through the chamber. A sudden stream of light at once intense and soft floods the interior of the ventricle, then withdraws calmly, like a wave, pacified.

The organ contracts and thuds once more. A second breath of light fills the heart, which begins to beat.

\* \* \*

The heartbeats melt into the thrumming whump of the helicopter's blades. Enveloped in a flurry of smoke and dust, Evan sits against his tree. Scattered on the ground around him are the CD player, the used-up batteries, the emptied sachets of freeze-dried food, the upturned gourd. Wrapped in Tsepel's tunic, he holds on firmly to the box of matches. It is empty. In front of him, where Anne's body used to be, a fire is raging. The branches gathered by the old man are burning.

An Indian in a safety helmet emerges from the thick cloud and calls out.

'He is here!'

He approaches at a run, followed by another crew member carrying a stretcher.

'I am very glad we are finding your good self! We are having much trouble – it is very good you are lighting a fire.'

The rescuers lift Evan onto the stretcher. They set off at once. Evan watches the scene fly past: the mangled motorbike, the disembowelled backpack, the scattered effects, Tsepel's 'spot'. No trace of

Anne remains. Only a few charred strips of sleeping bag fly up from the burning charcoal, ashes spinning in the air.

The paramedic shouts over the sound of the helicopter, 'You will be all right, sir. Do not be worrying.'

The din in the cabin is appalling. The helicopter escapes up into the clear sky.

'The old man . . .'

The medic leans over Evan.

'What old man?'

Evan struggles to speak.

'Where's the old man?'

The rescuer straightens in surprise and looks at Evan.

'An old man, he is here?'

Evan hasn't the strength to answer. He looks away. Outside, bathed in the last golden rays of the sun, the snow-capped mountaintops gleam. The helicopter swings between two peaks, into the sun, and enters the blinding light.

# Die? Whatever For?

*Mankind, having failed to remedy death, misery and ignorance, resolved, for the sake of its happiness, never to think about them.*

(Blaise Pascal, 1623–62)

*Write about death? It won't sell. No one wants to think about it. It won't find a readership. Nobody cares!*

As absurd as it may be, death is a taboo subject in most Western countries. We hide from it and avoid it for as long as possible. As with serious illnesses and accidents, it's one of those things we like to imagine happen only to other people; after all, we've got more important things to be getting on with.

Paradoxically, usually it isn't death itself that is the problem, nor, for that matter, what does or does not follow it. It is the conditions of death and the suffering that ensues, whether physical or psychological, which frighten us most.

These fears seem to be reinforced by the sense

that many people die badly. Over-medicalisation, unremitting therapy, lengthening life expectancy, families spread far and wide – all these factors bring new issues. Aside from the pain attached to illness or physical decline, the dying suffer from loneliness, a sense of abandonment, lack of communication and denial of their imminent deaths by medical personnel, by members of their families and by society in general. But why?

Tormented by our careers, trapped by our material needs, monopolised by domestic worries, most of the time we let our lives pass in a hurry. Even the retired run around, fleeing the boredom that we associate with the end of work, throwing themselves into all sorts of new activities. For they are afraid of being useless, of serving no purpose if they don't keep moving, don't reject encroaching death. Naturally, then, when the game suddenly stops, we are at a loss: 'Die? Already? How's that possible?'

Under these conditions, would it not make sense to ask: do we die badly because we live badly?

*The Tibetan Book of the Dead* describes the great voyage into death as a difficult ordeal but also, and above all, as an opportunity for liberation, a chance to find the bliss that was beyond us when we lived. The suffering and fear evoked in the book are essentially tied to *karma*, to the actions that we took or did not take in our lives and to their impact on our consciences.

People who work with the dying confirm how important the last days and hours are. All of a sudden, right before the end, the dying want to make peace with themselves, with others, with the world. 'He died peacefully,' we say to reassure ourselves. Dying in peace is important, certainly, but why not anticipate it? Is it so painful, so difficult to prepare oneself for death? Does this require the accumulation of knowledge, of experiences, a belief in God or in life after death?

What would you do if you were told that you had only one month to live?

Imagining our own death as imminent forces us to verify or evaluate the importance we attach to those things we impose on ourselves on a daily basis, month after month and year after year.

Imagining our own death as imminent obliges us to take stock of ourselves, of our choices and actions.

Imagining our own death as imminent brings to light what we hold dearest in our heart of hearts, what we truly value.

Imagining our own death as imminent means acknowledging the plenty in our lives.

Imagining our own death as imminent means considering freedom, a process that can revolutionise not only our individual existences but also society.

Might it not be these disturbing questions that encourage us to avoid thinking too much about death, and about our lives?

*The oil of my lamp*
*Is all used up, in the night.*
*At my window, the moon!*

(Bashō, 1644–94)

# Select Bibliography

## Books about *The Tibetan Book of the Dead* or Tibetan Buddhism

Blofeld, J. *The Tantric Mysticism of Tibet: A Practical Guide to the Theory, Purpose and Techniques of Tantric Meditation*. New York, Penguin, 1992 (new edn)

Bokar Rinpoche. *Death and the Art of Dying in Tibetan Buddhism*. San Francisco, Clearpoint Press, 1993

Fremantle, F., & Trungpa, C., trans. *The Tibetan Book of the Dead: The Great Liberation through Hearing in the Bardo*. Boston, Shambhala Publications, 2007 (new edn)

Sogyal Rinpoche, trans. *The Tibetan Book of Living and Dying*. San Francisco, HarperSanFrancisco, 1994

Thurman, R.A.F., trans. *The Tibetan Book of the Dead*. New York, Bantam Doubleday Dell, 1993

Trungpa, C. *Transcending Madness: The Experience of the Six Bardos*. Boston, Shambhala Publications, 1992

## Books about death and accompanying the dying

Ariès, P. *Western Attitudes toward Death: From the Middle Ages to the Present*. Baltimore, The Johns Hopkins University Press, 1975

Kubler-Ross, E. *Living with Death and Dying*. New York, Scribner, 1997 (new edn)

Levine, S. & O. *Who Dies? An Investigation of Conscious Living and Conscious Dying*. New York, Anchor, 1989 (new edn)